A COMPROMISE WITH DEATH

The Narn held the sword up for Vir's closer inspection.

"It's not for you—but it will be if you don't listen closely," the Narn hissed.

The iron grip tightened; the sword edge glinted in caught nightlight.

"Listen carefully, Vir Cotto. We have Londo Mollari, and we will not release him until G'Kar is set free. Do you understand that?"

"You have to let Londo go!" Vir blurted out. "And you can't free G'Kar!"

The blade came very close to Vir's face; the edge ticked his nose. "What did you say? Repeat it, and die on this street!"

"Ummm, never mind. Perhaps another time."

"The next time we meet you will die, unless you heed my warning. Free G'Kar, and perhaps Londo Mollari will live."

"Perhaps?" Vir said in a meek voice.

"Perhaps."

Then the Narn dropped Vir in a heap on the street, and was gone. . . .

Look for

in your local bookstore

BABYLON 5:

PERSONAL AGENDAS

by
Al Sarrantonio

Based on the series by
J. Michael Straczynski

A Dell Book

Published by
Dell Publishing
a division of
Bantam Doubleday Dell Publishing Group, Inc.
1540 Broadway
New York, New York 10036

ISBN: 0-440-22351-2

Printed in the United States of America

Published simultaneously in Canada

May 1997

10 9 8 7 6 5 4 3 2 1

For Chris Vardeman:
One day, maybe, a real Space Cadet

Grateful acknowledgment is made to
J. Michael Straczynski,
who provided the idea, as well as the title,
for this book.

Historian's note: The events of this novel take place in 2261, before the episode "Falling Toward Apotheosis."

CHAPTER 1

SEVENTY-FIVE human light-years.

When G'Kar thought of it in those terms, as years made of pure light, it somehow didn't seem so far. It seemed . . . almost elegant.

But still depressing.

Seventy-five human light-years.

The distance from Babylon 5 to the despised planet Centauri Prime.

And how far was Narn from Babylon 5?

G'Kar knew this intimately: a little over 10 Narn light-years, which equaled . . . yes, 12.2 human light-years.

He distracted himself with other problems: the calculation of distance in Narn light-years from Babylon 5 to Earth, from Earth to Minbar, from Minbar to Narn . . .

And then there was another thought that distracted him:

How far was it in light-years from Narn to Centauri Prime?

G'Kar found himself gritting his teeth.

Not at the mathematics, which involved simple

calculations and conversions that the former Narn ambassador to Babylon 5 knew all too well.

The problem of the distance between Narn and Centauri Prime was the easiest of all to answer, because the answer involved no mathematics at all.

In fact, G'Kar was able to calculate it now, as he gritted his teeth in pain as the latest lash of the whip (a conventional one, the "electro-whip" being reserved for "special" occasions) held by one of Centauri Emperor Cartagia's pain technicians bit into his back, as the evil emperor himself sat looking at G'Kar with fading amusement from a resplendent red throne.

As the emperor let out a full-fledged yawn, not bothering to cover his mouth, the whip cracked once again, driving hot pain into G'Kar's raw back and making him try even harder to take his mind from the agony by thinking of mathematics problems.

How far was it from Narn to Centauri Prime?

Answer: *The distance of hatred*.

CHAPTER 2

IN the torture room, Emperor Cartagia was bored.
Stifling yet another yawn, he waved his hand at
the pain technician and the lashing of the Narn
G'Kar immediately stopped. The proud savage tried
to show no emotion, keeping his eyes fixed on the
emperor, but Cartagia noted a slight relaxation in his
frame, which momentarily lifted the emperor's
boredom. He made a slight motion with one finger,
hoping G'Kar hadn't seen, and the torturer immediately cracked his whip once more, making the Narn
nearly cry out in pain.

So he hadn't expected it!

Splendid!

But now the Narn stood proud once more, needing no pillory post, merely shackled, refusing to collapse after a solid hour of conventional lashing, and
Emperor Cartagia felt boredom crawl into him to
stay.

Not bothering to stifle his biggest yawn yet, he
waved the prisoner away.

"Take him back to his cell—and don't feed him

today,'' the emperor said, thinking perhaps to drop by later to see how the Narn was faring.

If he wasn't still bored.

As the pain technician bowed and backed away, two imperial guards immediately flanked the former Narn ambassador to Babylon 5, and led him away.

He wouldn't allow himself to be dragged, even with the whipping he had sustained.

Catching sight of the blood lines on the Narn's back, the emperor was suddenly shaken out of his boredom.

He thought of calling the guards back—perhaps even rising from his throne to administer a lashing to the Narn himself.

He began to rise—but then another yawn rose into his throat and he dropped back into the throne.

Bored.

Thirsty.

''More wine!'' he cried, as a half-dozen retainers scrambled for flagons to attend to him.

The latest yawn was replaced by a chuckle. He thought of his uncle, the late Emperor Turhan, who had always seemed so stern in the job. Why, the old fool had even, on occasion, removed his wig and conducted business in front of others without his hair!

Scandalous!

And stupid!

As if he didn't care about what others thought of him, or the trappings of his exalted position!

As his glass was filled by a lackey, the emperor brushed a hand over his own beautiful and stylishly short (he knew it was stylish because he had come up with the idea himself) fringe of hair.

Why, this was power!

And what good was power without . . . amusement!

He brought the wine to his lips, tasted, then drank it down.

"Bring me . . . amusement!" he cried.

And waited for the next act in his daily play.

CHAPTER 3

A SLAVE is not always a slave.

Five Narns, newly arrived slaves from their mother planet, were led with the ninety others from their slave ship through city streets unfamiliar to them. The manifest that had accompanied them said that all of them, the full ninety-five, were accomplished tunnel workers, good at laying water and sewer lines, but this was only true for ninety of them.

The special five were good at other things.

For a while, the ninety-five stayed tightly together, herded like cattle through unknown streets under light from a strange sun. Some were spat upon by passing Centauri and crude jokes were directed their way. At one point, one of the five who were not in truth tunnel workers was hit with something thrown from a building, which hit his cheek. He did not flinch, and the object did not cut the skin.

The slaves' overseers, looking forward to rest and relaxation before returning to Narn for another shipment of slaves, did their duty just before arrival at the tunnel site where the slaves were to be turned over, but were lax in their count; they counted ninety-six and, fed up with the exercise, decided to wait until after lunch for a second count; after all, one of them laughed, if it turned out there was an *extra* slave how could they get into trouble?

But when the second count was made an hour later, it was found that there were only ninety slaves, and that five were missing—five whose names somehow turned out to be impossible to trace . . .

So this was Centauri Prime.

L'Kan was not impressed, and, he knew, neither were his companions. Compared to what the Narn homeworld had been before the Centauri had first come, the lush forested beauty of a world that was only a memory now, this world was . . . decadent.

As he walked through the streets in his ragged slave's robe, his tall, burly build making his head stand out over his fellows, he took in the world of Centauri Prime. The overstated architecture, the rich adornments, the flowing robes and other overdone styles of dress, the flaunting of abundance—all decadent.

L'Kan imagined that it had always been this way.

There was not, however, much time for sightseeing. Five Narns unattended by a Centauri slave master would quickly be noticed and reported.

It was time for them to make themselves . . . disappear.

For they had a mission to accomplish.

CHAPTER 4

COMPLICATIONS, complications.

Sometimes, even Londo Mollari got tired of complications.

Life, of course, was complications; Londo knew that. There were the complications of rank, and status, and power. And there were the complications of dress, and presentation, and cunning. And there were social complications, of marriage (Londo made a face, thinking of his three wives, Timov, Daggair, and Mariel, whom he referred to as "Famine, Pestilence, and Death"). And there were complications that all of these complications seemed to create.

And then there were the complications that seemed to wait on his breakfast plate each morning: the new complications.

Like today's, for instance.

Like Vir.

"Drinking your breakfast today?" Vir said, not hiding his disapproval. Londo's protégé never failed to annoy him, yet Londo never failed to feel a certain sense of . . . comfort, almost, when the younger man was around. He had no idea if his instincts were truly paternal—or if Vir's underlying honesty and decency were merely useful on occasion.

Probably the latter.

With a sprinkle of the former.

More complications . . .

"Yes, Vir," Londo said, raising his glass in a sarcastic toast to the younger man, "I *am* drinking my breakfast. And I may drink my lunch and dinner also—with a few snacks in between."

Vir fairly clucked. "You need all your wits about you, Londo. You know it may cloud your judgment—"

"My judgment is fine with or without imbibing!" Londo remarked testily. "And I do not need you to lecture me!"

Vir gave a disapproving frown. "It's just that—"

"Stop!" Londo pushed his glass aside, noting with some satisfaction that it was nearly empty anyway. "There, I will not drink any more of it. Does that make you happy?"

Vir, letting his frown soften a bit, responded, "Yes."

"Good. Then now we can get down to business. What is it that is so important?"

Rubbing his hands nervously, Vir said, "G'Kar needs to see you in his cell. Immediately. And alone. I've taken the liberty of checking his cell for listening or recording devices, and made sure guards loyal to you will be placed around it when you are there."

"And what is so important that I should deign to visit G'Kar in his cell?" Londo asked.

"He said it was very important. That . . ."

"Well?"

Vir looked very worried, which was always a clue that further complications were about to emerge. "He said your plan might be in jeopardy."

"What!"

"He said . . ."

Londo felt his blood beginning to boil; he wanted very much to drain the glass he had recently pushed away. "Tell me exactly what he said!"

Vir took a couple of breaths and tried to calm down. "G'Kar said that if steps were not taken immediately, then everything you and he are working toward will be . . ."

Barely able to control his apprehension now, Londo shouted, "What word did he use, Vir?"

Looking at the floor, Vir whispered, "Kablooey."

"Kablooey?" Londo repeated, startled. "What does 'kablooey' mean?"

"Apparently it is an Earth term, one G'Kar learned from Captain Sheridan. It means . . . kaput."

Totally flustered now, Londo raised his hands in the air. "And what does 'kaput' mean, Vir!"

"It means . . ."

Once again, Vir hesitated.

"Tell me now, or I will have you flogged!" Londo shouted, losing all patience. *"Better yet,"* he snarled, casting his eyes about for something to hit the younger man with, *"I will flog you myself!"* To himself, Londo thought, *I'm getting carried away;*

the emperor's madness must be rubbing off on me . . .

Vir took a step back, but recovered. Londo noted that the younger man was marking the position of the door, and how far it was away from him.

"It means 'out the window,' 'finito,' or 'bye-bye.' In other words, terminated."

"Get out!" Londo yelled, reaching for a nearby gewgaw to throw. But Vir had already made it to the door and was gone.

Londo was alone again.

With more complications.

Breathing normally now, he furrowed his brow and began to ponder.

So: something was threatening his grand plan—threatening to dash to bits everything he had been working for and, perhaps, end his life in the bargain.

Something was threatening to make Londo Mollari "kablooey."

"I think not," Londo said, to no one in particular except himself, as he drew the glass on his breakfast table back toward him, lifted it to his lips, and drained it dry.

CHAPTER 5

In the Observation Dome of Babylon 5, Captain John Sheridan, never short of worries, was concentrating now on one in particular.

"Is there any possibility we could get Mollari back here now, perhaps on some pretense? I'm sure he would be easier to deal with face-to-face."

Commander Susan Ivanova shook her head. "No, Captain. He's refused every 'invitation,' no matter how it's been phrased." She smiled slightly. "I even tried telling him that his favorite bar in the Zocalo got in a special shipment of his favorite spirits, but would only hold it for him for three days. That was four days ago."

Sheridan slammed his fist into the palm of his opposite hand. "There's got to be something we can do!"

"Nothing at the moment, sir."

"The thought of G'Kar rotting away on Centauri Prime, while we do nothing, just makes me sick."

"It makes all of us sick, Captain."

"And Garibaldi doesn't have any tricks up his long sleeve?"

"The plain fact is that once G'Kar left Babylon 5, he essentially left our protection behind. He knew that, we knew that."

At that moment, Sheridan's link chimed.

"Sheridan here," the captain said, lifting it toward his mouth.

"Garibaldi here," the security chief's voice responded. "I've got some news about G'Kar."

"Good news, I hope?" Sheridan asked.

"Could be. But I don't think I should talk about it over a link."

"Meet me in my office in five minutes," Sheridan said. He signed off and turned to Ivanova. "Want to come along?"

"Wouldn't miss it for the world," the commander replied.

In five minutes exactly, Chief Garibaldi sauntered into the captain's office. His slight smile gave Sheridan hope.

Sitting behind his desk, Sheridan looked up. "Well?"

Garibaldi cocked his head. "I've got . . . good news, and bad news."

Sheridan shook his head, and Ivanova, seated in a chair turned toward Garibaldi, groaned.

Sheridan said, "Give us the good news first."

Garibaldi still wore his slight smile. "Sure. The good news is that the Centauri are still transferring slaves from the Narn homeworld to Centauri Prime."

"That's *good* news?" Commander Ivanova blurted, her eyes widening.

"Sure is," Garibaldi said. "Because five of the latest shipment of slaves are Narn soldiers sent there to find G'Kar and free him."

Captain Sheridan gave a wry smile himself. "That *is* good news," he admitted.

"But what's the bad news?" Ivanova demanded.

"Well," Garibaldi answered, "the bad news is that there's nothing we can do to help them. My . . . source tells me that these five guys are very good, but that once they're on Centauri Prime they're on their own. If you want more good news, these Narn have sworn to die for their mission, and there's nothing in the world that will keep them from doing what they were sent there to do."

"I wish there was something *we* could do!" Sheridan declared earnestly.

"So do I," Garibaldi agreed. "I hate having my hands tied like this. But for the life of me, I don't know what we can do."

CHAPTER 6

G'KAR was thinking of home.

It helped to pass the time in his cell, and it also took his mind from the pain he felt. Thinking pleasant thoughts helped keep the deep lashes in his back from reminding him of very unpleasant things indeed. His back felt as if it were on fire—which was decidedly *not* pleasant.

Specifically, he was thinking of a very distinct scenario on the Narn homeworld. Under an angry sky that had once been beautiful but now reeked of destruction, against a backdrop of burned buildings in a city that had once been beautiful, G'Kar was playing a game in his mind. In the game he shot a PPG rifle at a piece of fruit that rested upon the head of Emperor Cartagia, who had been brought to Narn in chains, much as G'Kar himself had been brought to Centauri Prime.

In the fantasy, the emperor, dirty, disheveled, his ridiculous fringe of hair sticking out at all angles, his robes torn and filthy, stood against a broken, blackened wall of what had once been a resplendent residence. In fact, it had once been G'Kar's boyhood

home. And resting upon the emperor's fringe of ridiculous flattened hair was the smallest piece of fruit
G'Kar could imagine. He had first heard of this
game from Security Chief Garibaldi on Babylon 5:
someone in ancient Earth history named William
Tell had become a legend by playing just such a
game. He had used an Earth apple and had shot it
from his own son's head.

But in G'Kar's fantasy version, an apple was
much too large a piece of fruit to use. He needed
something more . . . challenging, so perhaps he
would use a . . . raisin. Yes, another Earth fruit,
but of more appropriate size.

And then G'Kar stood back twenty paces and attempted to shoot the raisin from Emperor Cartagia's
head.

And every time, as Cartagia cringed and
squeaked for mercy, G'Kar's shot was just a little
too low . . .

"Oops," G'Kar said softly, smiling to himself.

"What do you have to smile about, G'Kar?"
came the harshly sarcastic voice of Londo Mollari,
who now stood before him in his cell.

G'Kar, sitting with his back against the hard wall
of the cell, pulled himself from his reverie and for a
moment was torn by two unpleasantries: the return
of the pain in his back, and the sight of the despised
Londo, dressed in a red-and-white robe.

He overcame his disgust by concentrating on the
business that had to be conducted in this room.

Arms folded in front of him, Londo demanded,
"Well? What was so important that I had to be
dragged from my morning meal?"

G'Kar smiled slightly. "No one dragged you, Mollari. You came running like an Earth dog when you heard that your precious plans might be in jeopardy."

Londo flushed with anger and for a moment said nothing.

"We both know why you're here," G'Kar continued, unable to keep himself from digging into Mollari.

To G'Kar's surprise, Londo's tone evened.

"Yes, I suppose we do," Mollari assented. "So why don't we just get to business, then?"

"Because I'm having so much fun *before* we get to business," G'Kar said, unable to stop jabbing at the other. For emphasis he turned slightly to show Mollari his latest wounds, and it was with some satisfaction that he noted Londo winced.

"There's nothing I can do about that," Londo responded, almost quietly. "We both know how important it is to keep up appearances in your captivity. As evil as you think I am, I would, for the sake of our bargain, have you better treated if I could. I certainly don't want you to die—at least not until our bargain is consummated. The Emperor . . . is amused by doing these things. When he is gone—"

"When he is gone will you be any different, Mollari?" G'Kar asked quietly.

"I've given you my word!" Londo spat back.

"Yes," G'Kar countered, "you've given me your word that when and if I help you rid yourself of Emperor Cartagia—not that I would need much urging at that point—Narn will be freed from Centauri rule. But when that time comes, Mollari, will you have me flogged for *your* amusement?''

"Such things will never *amuse* me, G'Kar," Londo sneered. "But if ever I would have anyone flogged, let me assure you that it would most certainly be you."

G'Kar started to laugh, until the pain in his back prevented him. "I'm sure it would."

Suddenly thoughtful, Mollari said, "You know, G'Kar, our history is a long and hateful one, yours and mine, but as far as I know we have always been honest in our hatred. When you blackmailed me in 2257 with evidence of my grandfather's . . . indiscretions during our first occupation of Narn, I believe the rules of our . . . relationship were set in stone."

"Yes," G'Kar said, "and when you refused to give me my G'Quan Eth plant for my ceremony—"

"In retaliation for the Narn treatment of my nephew!"

G'Kar looked at his old nemesis for a moment, and then smiled grimly.

"It seems we could go on all day in this vein," he murmured quietly.

"All day and all night, and then another day and night after that," Mollari said, holding the other's gaze.

"Then perhaps we should get to business," G'Kar suggested.

"Yes," Mollari countered, "we should."

"I have . . . learned," G'Kar began, "that a small band of Narns has arrived on Centauri Prime with the express purpose of freeing me."

"What!" Londo exploded, then caught himself and lowered his voice, leaning closer. "If that were to happen," he hissed, "then everything we've worked for will be ruined!"

"Precisely." G'Kar nodded. "And that is why they must fail."

Londo was almost in awe of the other's conclusion. "You impress me, G'Kar. And, I must say, for the very first time. That you would sacrifice your own people—"

"I will not sacrifice them," G'Kar replied. "If anything happens to these men, our deal is the only thing that will be sacrificed. I want them removed without being hurt. They are brave soldiers, and sworn to their task, of that you can be sure. But they must not be harmed."

"And how do you propose that I do that?" Londo inquired. He waved his arms. "Shall I broadcast a message throughout all of Centauri Prime that the five cutthroat Narn dogs who have wormed their way here to murder Centauri citizens should just forget what they came here for and quietly go home?"

"How you accomplish it is your problem, Mollari," G'Kar said stoically. "Only believe me when I say that these patriots will come to no injury on my behalf. If so, I will terminate our agreement."

"You are a fool! To sacrifice all that I promised you for a few men is madness!"

"Nevertheless, it is what I pledge. If it were my own life, I would gladly give it. But I will not let others die for me."

Stifling his anger, Londo threw his hands up and

turned toward the cell door. "Then I will do what I can to uphold your madness. Because I believe you are insane enough to do what you say." He turned back to regard his enemy. "Is there anything else you can tell me about them? Where they are? Who they are?"

"I have told you all I know. If I learn more—"

"How did you learn even this much?" Londo broke in, suddenly fascinated.

G'Kar smiled thinly. "I have sources that I could not trust you with."

"Fine. But in the meantime, may your wounds be slow to heal."

"In all matters, we shall see," G'Kar uttered cryptically.

Muttering to himself, Londo left the cell. In a moment there was a clang as the door was closed, leaving G'Kar once more alone with this thoughts.

The pain in his back returned, making him wince, but he quelled it with his mind game, conjuring up his image of a Centauri with a tiny bit of fruit on his head, and he, G'Kar, back twenty paces with a PPG rifle whose aim was just a bit off on the low side, putting a deadly shot in between the eyes of the Centauri.

Only this time it was not Emperor Cartagia, but Londo Mollari.

CHAPTER 7

L'Kan and his four fellow Narn soldiers found their training in tunneling immediately useful.

Knowing that unescorted Narns would last on the surface of the planet for an amount of time measured in minutes, the five immediately headed for a tunnel project at the edge of the city. Still wearing their chains, they were able to look absorbed and unobtrusive; they kept to the sides of buildings, walking with bowed heads behind a Centauri when possible. There was one tight spot when they met a contingent of Centauri imperial guards—but luck was with them and they fell into step behind a woman and her son just as the guards passed. The boy even unwittingly helped by turning and ordering them down, shouting, "On the street with you—now!"

They instantly obeyed, getting up only when the guards had safely passed; the boy was sticking his tongue out at them and L'Kan had to refrain from patting him on the head as the boy's mother pulled him away, saying with disgust, "Don't touch them, dear—they may be dirty."

But their plan had been a good one, and before

long they found themselves in an underground passage that led to a wider series of passages, some of which branched out to cover most of the city underground.

When they had finally reached their hiding place, a nearly empty and little-used storage area with rock walls and two ways in and out, L'Kan said, "We will rest, and refresh ourselves, and then we will plan our attack."

"When can we kill our first Centauri?" one of his companions asked, pulling his knife from its sheath and examining it with a kind of hunger.

"We will kill no Centauri unless it is necessary," L'Kan snapped. "And I will kill any of you who defy me in this." His harsh tone softened. "I know how all of you feel: you are finally on the enemy's soil and want to strike at his heart. But believe me, what we are here for will hurt him far more than a few cold Centauri bodies. If we are able to snatch G'Kar out from under their noses it will prove to everyone that Narn is unbeaten, and that no one is safe from our wrath."

"Limited as it is," another of his companions muttered with disgust.

L'Kan straightened. "Limited as it is. But it will not always be so. All of us have lost members of our families and good friends. None of us have been immune to what has happened to our people. But as we rose up once before, we will again. No matter how long it takes."

He glowered at his companions, one by one.

"Am I clear in this? No blood will be spilled unless it is necessary to accomplish our mission.

And make no mistake about it: accomplish our mission we will. Nothing will stand in our way.''

One by one they nodded.

L'Kan's eyes narrowed, and his voice became a hiss.

''But one day it will be different, and then perhaps there will be a river of Centauri blood where we stand today.''

To this, none of his soldiers objected.

CHAPTER 8

Vir Cotto could not remember the last time he had had a good sleep. He felt perhaps it had been years. Certainly not on his recent visits to Babylon 5.

And certainly not since he had come home from Babylon 5, to this latest madness.

He lay in bed, staring at the ceiling, while a breeze blew the curtains. It felt as if it might rain. Vir had enjoyed rain when he was a boy—he remembered once slipping away when very young when a rainstorm broke over the Imperial Palace as his father was doing business at the top of the steps near the entrance; Vir stared at the spatterings of raindrops in the huge rectangular water gardens in front of the palace and could not help himself. Before his father realized, the young boy had run down the steps and was splashing in the shallow water, his face turned up to receive the wet gift from the sky.

When he looked up, there was Emperor Turhan himself staring at him, from outside the artificial pond.

"You know, boy, I have half a mind to join

you,'' the emperor had said while the boy quaked in sudden fear at his indiscretion; but the emperor merely waved away the approaching imperial guards, and Vir's father.

"Let him play," Emperor Turhan had ordered.

As soon as the emperor was gone, Vir's father had hauled him out of the pond and spanked him, but even through his tears the image that Vir never forgot was the look of longing on Emperor Turhan's face.

I have half a mind to join you . . .

Now Vir was beginning to understand what the emperor had meant. In many ways it was much easier being a child than a grown-up, and there had been times recently when Vir wished he were that young boy again, playing in that rain-spattered pond. It would be worth the beating he had gotten just to feel that sense of abandonment from care, of pure joy, which he had felt for those few precious moments . . .

"Ah, well," Vir said, to no one but himself; such things were for children, and other things were for . . . nonchildren.

He closed his eyes, for perhaps the hundredth time that night, seeking sleep, but only jumbled thoughts came.

In the midst of them came an image of Lyndisty.

For a moment he smiled his saddest smile. There, indeed, was a mixture of childhood and adulthood if ever there was one. His wife-to-be was both child and adult to Vir—a child in so many ways, yet very much an adult in some of her hardened views, especially on the harsh treatment of the Narn homeworld and its inhabitants. Vir did not like the fact that she considered the Narn little more than animals, or worse.

And yet, when he thought of her Vir felt warm, thinking of her childlike side . . .

"You have been avoiding me, Vir."

Vir was startled—her voice sounded so *real* . . .

"It's not right to ignore your bride-to-be," Lyndisty's soft voice continued. "You don't really want to keep me away, do you?"

Vir opened his eyes and saw the curtains rustling against the window—all except one of them, which was still, as if a figure were behind it.

"Lyndisty?" Vir said in alarm, sitting up in bed.

For a moment there was silence, and Vir began to rub his eyes, thinking he must have been dreaming; but then Lyndisty's voice said, "Yes, Vir."

She stepped from behind the curtain.

"Lyndisty!" Vir cried, bunching the bedcovers up under his chin modestly.

She smiled in amusement and moved closer into his bedroom.

"I've wanted to see this room since I learned you were back on Centauri Prime," she said, still smiling as she looked around. "It's very nice. I like what you've been able to do with the furnishings in such a short time." She picked up a nearby vase from its pedestal.

"I—I—" Vir began, looking around as if he had been caught in something illegal. "I would have cleaned! I would have had my tunic pressed!"

"Nonsense!" She laughed, brushing his face with her soft hand as she passed him, still curious at her surroundings. She ran a hand over the ornate frame of a painting that hung near the bed.

"But you should not be here!" Vir cried. "It isn't right! Or proper!"

"It isn't right or proper that you have avoided me, Vir, dear," Lyndisty countered, turning a slight frown on him.

"I—I—no! You're right! And if you'll just leave now, I promise to call on you tomorrow!"

Her frown turned into a smile. "But that won't be necessary, Vir! For I'm here now!"

As she approached the bed, Vir's face froze in panic; he pulled the covers even tighter up around his chin.

"You—you—really shouldn't be here!"

"You're right, Vir, I shouldn't," she said coyly. "But I am."

She stopped before him. The smooth, shaved skin of her scalp set off her large, dark eyes so beautifully that Vir nearly swooned. He was so *confused*.

"What . . . do you want?" Vir croaked, as she leaned forward, as if to kiss him.

Her smile widened, and Vir gasped as she opened her mouth. He puckered his mouth stiffly in anticipation of her kiss.

But instead he heard her voice.

"I only want to tell you, Vir, dear, that Mother and Father have invited you to our home. They feel it is time to meet you. They are throwing a gala in your honor, in five days."

Frozen with confusion, Vir opened his eyes and choked out, "Oh?"

Lyndisty's smile was even warmer.

"You will be there, won't you, Vir?"

"Well, I—"

"You wouldn't disappoint my parents, would you?"

And now she did kiss him, lightly, but if anything it only increased Vir's confusion.

Her eyes were so . . . *large* . . .

So . . . *beautiful* . . .

"Of course I'll be there!" he squeaked, smiling stiffly.

"Wonderful!" Lyndisty exclaimed, pecking him again on the lips and then turning, while Vir, trying to realize what he had done, stayed in position, his silly smile frozen on his face.

Suddenly he realized *what* he had just said.

"Lyndisty!" Vir cried out, but when he looked she was gone, and the curtains were blowing again, and no one stood behind any of them.

CHAPTER 9

CAPTAIN Sheridan was restless.

It wasn't as if he didn't have enough trouble to keep him busy. There was plenty of that. There were always big decisions to be made—about the Shadows, the Vorlons, about Babylon 5 itself—about everything, it seemed.

He was tired of big decisions.

Actually, he thought, as he readied himself for sleep, *it would be nice to have some minor details to preoccupy me for a while.*

Oh well, he thought. *Time for bed.*

He was tired enough, and when he did climb into his bed his weariness turned quickly to sleep.

And, as often happens, his sleep turned to dreams, in which what was really bothering him made itself manifest . . .

He was on a blasted reddish planet, which he could tell had once been fertile but now was not. The sky was sickly orange, the landscape a blasted plain of open sores and ruined buildings. Some of the buildings had once been magnificent, but were now cratered and pitted; not one stood as tall as it had been built.

The air was filled with dust, which looked as if it might never settle to the ground again. Sheridan coughed, and then he heard someone else cough and turned to see a figure just disappearing behind a battered building and out of sight.

In his dream, Sheridan tried to call out, but found that he could not speak.

Again he heard the other cough, and now Sheridan ran to the point where the other had disappeared: it was a street, wide but choked with debris, lined with half-toppled buildings.

At the end of it he saw the elusive figure—tall and stately—just turning another corner.

Again Sheridan tried to call out, unsuccessfully; but now he quickly ran on.

Breathing heavily, he reached the far corner just in time to see the figure again turn another corner—but closer this time.

Again Sheridan ran; again the figure turned, but closer, and then closer, in a tightening square—

And then Sheridan turned to see the figure—G'Kar—standing behind him, for they had tightened the square to the point where they met—and G'Kar, grim and proud, with pain-filled eyes, said, "Yes, Captain, I have been standing behind you all along—"

Captain Sheridan awoke with a start, and sat up in bed. It was as if he had not been asleep at all.

Yes, he thought, *I know what I have to do.*

He knew he should have done it to begin with.

In a moment he was out of bed, and in front of the communications screen in his quarters.

Delenn's face on the screen looked sleepy.

"John?" she said, stifling a yawn. "Is something wrong?"

"I'm sorry, Delenn, but I have to see you. Immediately."

Her sleepiness seemed to vanish. "Is it the Shadows or Vorlons?"

"No. But it's very important, nevertheless. Actually," he admitted, "perhaps it could have waited, but it's just that—"

She smiled knowingly.

"I have watched you the past day, John, and I noted a certain . . . restlessness."

"Well, yes," he agreed. "And now I know what it was from."

"Of course I'll come to you," she said, and smiled.

"Good. Thank you, Delenn."

As Sheridan signed off the screen, he muttered to himself, "Now we'll see how happy the others are to be rousted out of a sound sleep."

CHAPTER 10

"Don't be so foolish, Vir! Of course you must go to this party!"

"But I *can't*!" Vir said, waving his hands as he paced around Londo's office. Londo sat behind his huge desk, doing his best to ignore the younger man, which was difficult.

"Will you at least sit down!" Londo ordered.

"I can't sit! I can't eat! I can't *live*!" Vir moaned. He continued to pace, his eyes darting around the room as if he expected something to jump out at him from every opulently furnished corner.

"Nonsense, Vir! There is nothing that can't be dealt with!"

Stopping in his tracks, Vir looked at Londo hopefully.

"You'll intervene for me? Tell Lyndisty's parents I'm sick? Or better yet—that I'm dead?"

"Sit down, Vir, sit down," Londo urged, and Vir allowed himself to sink into the nearest chair. But still his face was hopeful.

"You'll get me out of this?"

"Of course not!"

Vir started to stand.

"Sit down, and stay down!" Londo ordered, and the sharpness of his command got through to Vir, who sank back into the seat and let out a groan.

"If you'll listen to me, Vir," Londo counseled, "I will get you through this."

"I don't want to get through it—I want to get *out* of it!"

"There is no way you can refuse an invitation to Lyndisty's parents' home," Londo said reasonably, "especially since you were already foolish enough to agree to go."

"I know . . ." Vir sighed.

"Her parents are heroes to all Centauri Prime, and to back out now would brand you not only as a fool but as a traitor. I myself would refuse to be seen with you ever again. You would be reviled in the streets—"

"Why is *everything* politics, Londo!" Vir wailed.

Mollari said impatiently, "Because it *is*."

"But her parents aren't heroes to *me*."

"Because they were responsible for thousands of deaths on Narn?" Londo asked.

"Yes! I can't accept that!"

"I suggest that you do," Londo said, his impatience resurfacing. "And I suggest you find something suitable to wear."

"But I don't want to go! I know what's going to happen! They're going to announce our marriage at this gala! I'll be trapped!"

Londo had suddenly settled back in his chair and was staring off into the distance thoughtfully.

"This is true, Vir. Once you are there you will be trapped, with nowhere to go. Believe me, I know these things. I've been through them myself. Have I told you about 'Famine, Pestilence, and Death'—"

"Yes! A thousand times! This is *me* we're worried about, remember?"

Londo's countenance had become even more thoughtful. "Perhaps there is a way after all to get you out of this gala before it happens."

Vir's face filled with hope, and he rose out of the chair and advanced to hover over Londo.

"Londo, I'll do anything. Scrub your floors. Anything . . ."

Lost in thought, in the possibilities of intrigue, Londo murmured, "Yes . . . That just might work . . ."

Vir clutched at Londo's tunic.

"Bless you, Londo! Bless you!"

"We'll see . . ." Londo said, still lost in plans.

CHAPTER 11

In the briefing room, surveying the mostly sleepy faces around him, Captain Sheridan said, "I've brought you all here because I don't think this is something that can wait until a reasonable hour."

Looking at his coffee mug and making a face, Security Chief Garibaldi concurred, "Neither can this coffee."

There were a few titters from the command staff mixed in with the yawns.

Sheridan smiled before proceeding. "I think we should help G'Kar directly," he said simply. *That woke them up,* he thought.

"Captain," Commander Ivanova interjected, "I'm sure I don't need to remind you that any assault on Centauri Prime would be considered a declaration of war. And the last thing Babylon 5 needs now is a war with anyone else."

"I agree," Sheridan said.

Delenn added, "And I must say directly, Captain, that any such action would be looked at with extreme severity by the Minbari government."

"I'm sure it would," Sheridan said. "And that's why I'm not talking about direct intervention."

He let that sink in for a few moments; it was Garibaldi who picked up on it first.

"You're . . . talking about covert action? A . . . spy-type thing?"

"Precisely," Sheridan replied. "I would ask for volunteers, and if they were caught they would disavow any connection with Babylon 5, or any government whatsoever."

"Wow," Dr. Stephen Franklin chimed in. "You're talking real cloak-and-dagger stuff here. Sounds like James Bond."

"Who?" Garibaldi asked.

"James Bond," Franklin explained, "was the hero of a series of twentieth-century Earth novels. He was always getting into impossible situations, and always getting out of them. Very smooth guy."

"I'm . . . familiar with the James Bond books," Sheridan said. "They were a bit silly, but enjoyable. The point here is," he continued, growing serious, "that G'Kar needs us. I had a dream not twenty minutes ago that told me why I've been feeling so restless and uneasy since I learned that he had been brought to Centauri Prime. In my dream G'Kar said to me, 'I'm standing behind you.' Basically, that's what he's always done. Even though the protection of his homeworld always came first, I can't think of a single instance where G'Kar was ready to sacrifice any of our lives to attain any of his goals. In his own way he's been a constant friend."

Sheridan's voice grew passionate. "And now he's been dragged to Centauri Prime in chains, and tortured, and humiliated. And I don't like that. I haven't liked it from the beginning. You'll remember that G'Kar got into this mess to begin with because he left Babylon 5 to look for one of us . . ." Sheridan looked at Garibaldi, who nodded grimly.

"I wish he hadn't done it," Garibaldi said. "But aren't you forgetting, Captain, that there's already a team of Narn commandos on Centauri Prime, trying to free G'Kar?"

"I know that. But they may not succeed. Or they may be able to use our help."

Sheridan looked in turn at Delenn, Garibaldi, Franklin, and Ivanova. "You all know how much Babylon 5, and the four of us in this room, have just gone through. Mr. Garibaldi and I are barely back from our recent . . . adventures. But I think I have a brief moment in time where we can do something for an old friend. It would be cruel of us to abandon him when we had any chance at all of helping. That's why, like I said, I'm asking for volunteers."

Instantly, four hands in the room went up. Sheridan, smiling, then raised his own. "I'm afraid, Commander, I'm going to have to ask you to stay and watch over things here. Ivanova opened her mouth as if to protest, then nodded.

"At this moment," he said, "I also wish G'Kar had never left Babylon 5. But he did. And even though we all know the risks, I say it's time for action."

"Damned straight," Garibaldi declared, and brought his fist down on the table.

CHAPTER 12

L'KAN waited impatiently for news.

He did not like this planet. Centauri Prime, which had never undergone the ravages that had befallen Narn, was, to L'Kan, an ugly place. Even its tunnels were ugly. Their hiding place was hung with ostentatious tapestries and furnished with overdone tables and chairs—and this an obscure storage area! And as to what little he had seen of the surface— well, he preferred the tunnels.

And the decadence of the Centauris was . . . astounding. They were a wasteful, vain people, taken to preening and infighting. Their hair, and the way they strutted, made them vile. To L'Kan's way of thinking, it must only have been a matter of luck that they had lasted this long.

Perhaps someday soon, they would know some of the hardships that the Narn homeworld had been subjected to.

Perhaps more could be accomplished here than was in the original plan . . .

Perhaps . . . L'Kan and his fellows could hurt the Centauri Republic to its core . . .

Wasteful thinking.

L'Kan banished such thoughts. His mandate had been clear and there would be no time for extras. He berated himself; after all, hadn't he given his men a speech decrying any deviation from plan?

Still, if things went wrong he would have to be flexible, wouldn't he?

Things will not go wrong.

But if they did . . .

Again, alone in his tunnel hideaway, perfecting his plans, waiting for his four soldiers to return, L'Kan pondered . . .

CHAPTER 13

IT had a gold seal, silver flourishes, and was ribbon-bedecked—and Vir held the invitation in his hand as if it were a snake.

Though he already knew what it said, he was loath to open the official document, fearing that once he did, there would be no backing out of what it contained. Though Londo had promised to help him, Vir suspected deep in his gut that nothing he did would prevent him from meeting Lyndisty's parents and being roped like a farm animal into the marriage he truly dreaded.

The very thought of it made him shiver.

How could he marry into such a family! Though they were deemed heroes, Lyndisty's parents, to Vir, could never be held in high esteem. They had made their reputations on the bones of thousands of Narns, and to Vir that was reprehensible.

Still, there were thoughts of Lyndisty's eyes—those beautiful orbs . . .

Vir sighed, then his gaze fell on the document he still held in his fingertips, and he dropped it to the floor.

Perhaps he would look at it later.

Perhaps not at all.

Gingerly, as if it might rear up and snap at him, he edged it away from him with his toe, until it slid beneath a chair and was hidden.

Perhaps later . . .

CHAPTER 14

FINALLY, L'Kan's men returned to the hiding spot. He could tell immediately that their reconnaissance mission had been a success. And nothing they told him led him to believe otherwise.

"We can strike at any time," Ra'Nik, whom L'Kan had named leader of the four, reported. As they sat around one of the room's ornate tables, there was a glow of anticipated victory in his eyes. "We even know exactly where his cell is." A note of contempt crept into his voice. "These Centauri are so soft, and so sure of their own invincibility, that they are lax about the comings and goings in their own prisons."

"How were you able to get so close?" L'Kan asked in some surprise. He had not anticipated that things would go this easily.

Ra'Nik sneered. "They make Narns do everything here for them. Any menial task is turned over to a Narn. We merely posed as janitors, and were allowed nearly free rein of the hallways."

"If you give a Narn a bucket and a mop on this

planet,'' one of his compatriots hissed, "he can go anywhere.''

"I am amazed," L'Kan said. "And also very pleased. Did you actually see G'Kar?"

"No," Ra'Nik reported. "He was not in his cell when we passed." He could not hide his anger. "The door was open, and his cell was stained with blood. From what we learned, he was being tortured at that moment, in front of Cartagia."

"Cartagia is a monster," L'Kan spat. "If only our mission were to assassinate him . . .''

"He is probably the only Centauri we could not get close to. He is surrounded night and day by imperial guards. He may be insane, but he is not stupid.''

"That is too bad," L'Kan snorted. "I would have liked to wring his neck myself.''

"Perhaps next time," Ra'Nik said. A sardonic smile came onto his face.

"Yes. But since things have gone so well, I suggest we complete this mission soon, so that there will be a next time.''

"When can we strike?" Ra'Nik asked.

"You have done well," L'Kan assented, studying the faces of the four men who had come with him.

Standing and turning away from them for a moment, L'Kan drew his *ka'toc* from its sheath, holding it up under one of the room's weak electric torchlights to study it for a moment before turning back to show it to his companions.

"You know what this means," he said. "Once I have taken this *ka'toc* from its sheath, I may not replace it until it has drawn blood. At this moment

G'Kar is tortured for the amusement of a madman. I say that he has spent his last day on Centauri Prime. We strike tonight.''

In the weak orange light, four other swords were drawn from four other sheaths.

CHAPTER 15

"WHAT do you mean, you haven't been able to get word to them?" Londo demanded. He paced G'Kar's cell as if it was entirely too small, which it was.

G'Kar, much the worse for wear after his most recent "audience" with Emperor Cartagia, sat on the floor with his back to the cell's rear wall, trying not to think about his most recent pain. His arms, which had been pierced with electric needles—some of them administered by the mad emperor himself— were unfeeling limbs that he could not even raise at the moment.

"When the time comes," G'Kar whispered, looking up at the pacing Mollari, "I think I shall very much enjoy carrying out your plan for Cartagia. I will make sure my arms work by then."

"But if you don't stop these soldiers who have been sent, we may not have that chance!" Londo complained, stopping to look down at the Narn.

"That is true. And as I told you, I have done

everything possible to get word to them. They cannot be stopped by anything I do.''

''What do you mean!'' Londo sputtered, turning his voice to a cautious whisper. ''I smuggled out a dictate in your own hand and had it delivered to Narn! Why don't they believe you?''

''Because it came via you, Mollari,'' G'Kar said slowly, in a low voice. ''They think it was tortured out of me. And besides, once these men have been dispatched, nothing can make them stop until they have completed their mission. That is why it is up to you, now, to stop them.''

''But how can I?''

G'Kar held Londo's stare. He tried to lift his hand to make a point, but the heat that coursed through it made him instantly reconsider.

''I will tell you what information I have, if you will pledge your life that they will not be harmed.''

''All right!'' Londo retorted, throwing up his hands. ''You have my pledge!''

''This is not a matter to take lightly, Mollari.''

Taking a deep breath, Londo said, ''Tell me what you know, and they will not be harmed. That is a promise I will keep, G'Kar.''

''They were smuggled in as miners,'' G'Kar said. ''I suggest you look in the tunnels.''

''Is that all? Do you realize how many tunnels there are?''

''That is all I know.''

Londo pulled in a long breath, then let it out slowly, as he thought. ''Very well. It is a start. And there are things that can be done.''

Londo turned to leave, and G'Kar found the strength to put a hand up, staying him.

G'Kar's stare was hard and fierce. "Find them. But if they are harmed . . ."

"I know," Londo said, without a trace of guile.

CHAPTER 16

From being restless two days before, Captain Sheridan suddenly found himself with all too much to do.

Suddenly, things were happening all over. Riots in Down Below had intensified. Lurkers held much of the level now and were threatening to expand their activities onto other levels. There were reports out of Garibaldi's office that passengers riding from one level to another were being extorted: if they didn't pay, they didn't get off where they wanted to.

And suddenly the Shadows, and Vorlons, were making noises again. There were rumors of impending action near the Euphrates sector; though unconfirmed, the reports were ominous.

Which meant another meeting, and a change of plans.

"After consultation with Delenn, we've decided that the two of us must remain on Babylon 5," Sheridan announced to his small audience in the briefing room: Ivanova, Garibaldi, and Franklin. "Therefore, I think the mission should be canceled. After all, it was my idea and I wouldn't feel right sending the three of you without me." He studied the three faces. "If you want to know the complete truth, I'm mad as hell that I can't do this, and the three of you have plenty to do here on Babylon 5."

Garibaldi said, "I'm already covered, Captain."

Franklin and Ivanova nodded, and then Ivanova spoke. "Captain, we talked this over before the meeting started, and we've already decided we want to go."

"In fact," Franklin added, "nothing you can say will change our minds. You have to stay here, but the fact remains that G'Kar needs help."

Sheridan straightened. He glowed with pride.

"We'll do you proud, Captain," Franklin said.

"I'm sure you will," Sheridan answered. "But now comes the hard part. You realize that if you're caught, or if anything happens to you, Babylon 5 can't take any responsibility for your actions?"

"We realize that, Captain," Ivanova said.

"In other words," Sheridan continued, "as far as we're concerned, you did this on your own—you understand that?"

"That's the way it has to be," Garibaldi said. "Whatever we do on Centauri Prime, it never happened."

"That's right," Sheridan said.

Franklin rose and proposed, "Captain, if that's all, I'll need these two here in Medlab for some . . . adjustments."

"I know what you mean," Sheridan agreed, smiling. "I can only tell you again that I wish I was going with you."

Garibaldi piped up, "Captain, I wanted you to

know that I looked up a few of those James Bond
novels Dr. Franklin was talking about. Actually,
they weren't bad. If you'd like, we could call you
'M.' '' Though Ivanova looked perplexed, Captain
Sheridan gave a small laugh.

''I appreciate the thought, but that won't be necessary.''

CHAPTER 17

In Medlab a few minutes later, Ivanova frowned and said, "Who's 'M'?"

Garibaldi turned to Franklin. "Should I tell her?"

"Sure. I'm busy anyway. I just hope my medical skills carry over into this area. It's been a long time since I was in a school play."

Garibaldi grinned and said to Ivanova, " 'M' was Bond's boss. There was another guy named 'Q' also, who was always coming up with all kinds of gadgets—"

"Hold still," Franklin said, applying a bit of glue to the top of Garibaldi's head.

When the doctor finished with Garibaldi, he began on Ivanova, who took a deep breath before letting him begin.

"You sure it's all right to do this?" Franklin asked. "It'll take months to grow back in."

"If it's the only way to do it right, then do it," Ivanova replied gamely. To deflect her thoughts, she turned to Garibaldi, who no longer looked quite like

Garibaldi. "So tell me more about this James Bond."

"Oh, he was quite the man. Had the ladies buzzing around him like flies—"

Ivanova made a face, which caused Franklin to scold, "Sit still!"

"—and everything he touched always turned out right," Garibaldi continued. "Let's see . . . he liked his martinis shaken, not stirred, usually wore a tuxedo, sometimes even to bed, and he fought a secret organization called SMERSH."

"Smersh?" Ivanova asked, skeptically.

Garibaldi frowned. "Well, it didn't sound so stupid when Ian Fleming wrote about it. But anyway, the guy never lost. And I bet he did look damned fine in that tuxedo."

"I always liked the not-losing part myself," Franklin mumbled, finishing up with Ivanova. He then started in on his own makeover, while Garibaldi and Ivanova looked at each other and shook their heads in wonder.

"Amazing," Ivanova said.

"Doc, you should have gone into trinocular films," Garibaldi said. "You could have made a mint as a makeup artist."

"I'm not so sure about that," Franklin said modestly, nearly done with his own disguise. He studied himself critically in a mirror. A pale-skinned, big-haired stranger stared back at him. "You two were easy. For me, the skin tone injections do most of the work."

"I still say it's amazing," Ivanova repeated.

And then Franklin was finished at his mirror, and

turned around to face his two companions, who
looked back at him as perfectly rendered Centauri:
Garibaldi in a Centauri tunic similar to Franklin's
own, his peacock fringe of hair nearly as fine as that
of Londo Mollari himself, and Susan Ivanova, bald
save for a ponytail, her large eyes beautiful under a
thin line of crown that circled her pate, and clothed
in the traditional robes of a Centauri woman.

CHAPTER 18

It was even easier for L'Kan and his men to get into the prison than it had been for Ra'Nik.

The tunnels that led directly beneath the prison had been more crowded with slave miners and Centauris during the day; this evening there was no one to avoid.

"They're brought back to their holding pens and cells at the end of the day," Ra'Nik said with barely disguised anger. "Some of them are worked until they die. There are stories of underfeeding and over-crowding; of unchecked disease; of beatings and sometimes executions." He made a fist. "When I think of what our people—"

L'Kan quieted him. "We all know of these things, and it makes all of us angry. There will come a time of reckoning. But for now, we must do what we were sent here for."

"I was just thinking," Ra'Nik said, "that if we could just free *some* of the slaves while we are here, that would be a small victory."

L'Kan's stare became more severe.

"Someday we will free them *all*," he pledged.

"Live for that day, Ra'Nik. Think of the weapon hidden in your legging, but do not use it until it is time."

After a moment the other nodded. "You are right." He gestured ahead. "Let's proceed."

In no time at all, they had ascended within the prison and had retrieved the janitor's equipment that Ra'Nik had hidden; with their ragged clothing, they were instantly transformed from a Narn commando team to a group of slave custodians making their nightly rounds.

They passed one sleepy Centauri guard and made their way to the floor where G'Kar's cell was located.

To Ra'Nik's surprise, there were no imperial guards about.

"There were at least two when we were here," he whispered to L'Kan, who held a bucket in one hand while fingering his hidden *ka'toc* in the other.

"Perhaps at night they are even more lax than during the day," L'Kan answered.

As they approached, there was a sound from the far end of the corridor; instantly they looked busy with mop and pail until two imperial guards passed, laughing between them. The Narns were given no notice whatsoever.

When the imperial guards had gone, L'Kan commanded, "Quickly!" and they advanced on G'Kar's cell.

"I can't believe it will be this easy!" Ra'Nik said, almost in glee.

"It won't be," L'Kan told him grimly, as they

stood before G'Kar's cell, which was empty, the door open.

Ra'Nik swore an oath.

"Are you sure this was the one?" L'Kan hissed.

"Yes!" Ra'Nik answered; he was backed up by the others.

"Perhaps the emperor is using G'Kar for his amusement," L'Kan mused; but then, studying the empty cell, he said, "No, that is not the case. G'Kar has been moved."

"How can you tell?" Ra'Nik asked.

The leader pointed to the floor. "It has been recently washed. And the rest of the cell cleaned. Didn't you tell me there were bloodstains from G'Kar's wounds when you were here?"

"Yes," Ra'Nik responded, his heart sinking. "Then we have failed."

"For the moment," L'Kan said. He fingered his *ka'toc*. "But we will not give up—"

There was another sound, more laughter, from the opposite end of the corridor: the two imperial guards returning.

"Quickly," L'Kan ordered. "We must leave the prison before any suspicion is aroused. There will be time to act again later."

Retrieving their buckets and mops, they hurried away from the approaching guards and were soon back in the tunnel beneath the prison.

CHAPTER 19

As they neared their hiding place beneath the city, L'Kan held up his hand for silence.

"Someone has been this way," he whispered.

He looked at the others. "Ra'Nik and I will go on," he said, still whispering. "The three of you will stay here and fight to the death if necessary." He held up his *ka'toc*.

The three nodded, baring their own swords.

L'Kan and Ra'Nik slipped quietly ahead.

Not only had their hiding place been discovered— but there was a contingent of imperial guards waiting for them.

But the Centauri guards were loud, and gave themselves away.

From his hiding place, L'Kan counted three guards, with two more stationed near the far exit of the underground chamber.

"We can kill them all," Ra'Nik hissed.

"And bring scores of them down here after us," L'Kan snapped.

Three guards near them howled with sudden laughter, and one said, "What did Mollari say? That he was sure they were down here?"

"He said he was *told* they were down here."

L'Kan drew his companion away into a shallow side tunnel.

"A traitor!" L'Kan hissed. "They know about our mission!"

"But who could have told them?" Ra'Nik demanded fiercely.

"No one can be trusted. It would be best for us—"

At that moment one of the three Centauri imperial guards who had been talking loudly walked by, froze, and stared into the alcove where Ra'Nik and L'Kan stood.

The Centauri's eyes widened.

"They're here!" the guard shouted.

The guard's two companions quickly appeared; but to L'Kan's surprise, as he and Ra'Nik stood ready to fight, they didn't draw weapons.

"We'll bring you in peacefully," one of the guards announced.

At that moment there was a shout, and L'Kan and Ra'Nik's three Narn companions appeared, swords ready, and charged the Centauri guards, who only at the last moment drew their weapons, while turning to flee.

Still shouting, the Narns chased the Centauris into the storage chamber they had been using as a hiding spot. L'Kan spotted the fifth and sixth Centauri guards at the far entrance, trying to flee, and before he could say anything Ra'Nik was past him, chasing them down.

L'Kan followed, after checking to see that his other Narn companions were not in need of help, which they were not.

In a very short while the battle was over, and the five Narn sheathed five *ka'toc* swords, all of which had tasted Centauri blood.

"Strange that they offered so little resistance," L'Kan commented.

"Yes," Ra'Nik answered. "But then, we gave them little time to think."

"And they *are* Centauri," one of the three companions added, drawing laughter from the other two.

"*Dead* Centauri, now!" one of the remaining two said, drawing more laughter.

But L'Kan was pensive. "There are bigger things to worry about now," he said. "For one thing, we have been discovered, and must keep on the move until we can find a new hiding place. And for another thing, we have not completed our mission. G'Kar still is in the hands of Cartagia, and has not been freed. And finally," he said, anger filling his voice, "someone has betrayed us."

"And that someone," said Ra'Nik, unsheathing his *ka'toc* once more, "will die."

CHAPTER 20

For two days Vir had avoided all forms of communication; had, in fact, hid in his quarters. If he hadn't felt silly doing it, he would have hidden in a closet.

However, in a moment of distraction, he now answered a communications screen summons, and found himself face-to-face (or, at least, screen-to-screen) with Lyndisty.

"Vir! Are you all right?"

"All right?" Vir nearly screeched in startlement. "Why wouldn't I be all right?"

"Well, for one thing you haven't been answering any of my messages. And for another, Mother and Father have yet to receive your acceptance of their invitation to come to our home!"

"Invitation?" Vir said, trying to look perplexed. "What invitation?"

"You mean you didn't receive it?" Lyndisty said, beginning to look upset.

"You mean a formal invitation was sent? Why . . ." Vir made a show of going through items in the immediate vicinity: papers, books, documents. He lifted objects to peer beneath, and then turned back to Lyndisty, smiling weakly, and shrugged.

"I . . . don't seem to have any such thing!"

Lyndisty was peering beyond him, and Vir realized to his horror that she was looking in the general direction of where he had pushed the invitation beneath a chair with his toe nearly two days before.

"Could that be it, on the floor beneath that chair?" Lyndisty asked with interest.

Knowing he was trapped, Vir turned with much show of surprise and looked at the spot she indicated.

"Why—whatever could this be!" he shouted in mock excitement, bending down to retrieve the ribboned and stamped envelope. He blew accumulated dust off it and winced.

"Could this be it?" he asked mildly, holding it up for Lyndisty's inspection.

"Yes!" she cried; and if she suspected him of intrigue she hid it well in her present excitement. "Then you'll come, Vir?"

"Why, those servants of mine will be flogged!" Vir rattled on, trying not to hear her. "To think that one of them would let such an important document fall to the floor and be kicked beneath a chair! Why, I'll beat them myself—!"

"Open it now!" Lyndisty coaxed, smiling.

"Now?" Vir echoed. "You mean, while . . . you're looking at me?"

"Of course!"

"Would that be . . . right?" he asked meekly.

"Why not? It's not as if it's our matrimony announcement, is it, Vir?"

Vir looked at her with abject shock and horror. "Did you say—"

"Open the invitation, Vir! Either that or just tell me now that you'll be there! It's in your honor, you know! Perhaps it will even be in . . . *our* honor, Vir!"

She was radiant, so much so that she must not have seen Vir's defenses leave him.

"I'll be there," he mumbled lifelessly.

"Oh, Vir, I can't *wait*!" she exclaimed, and then she signed off.

Emptied of strength, Vir sank into the chair under which the invitation had been hidden.

Sighing with resignation, he opened the invitation, just to make sure that it did not, indeed, hold an announcement of his impending nuptials.

With some relief, Vir saw that it did not; but he groaned nevertheless:

> *It is with great pleasure that Vir Cotto*
> *Is invited to a gala in his honor*
> *To be held at the residence of*
> *His bride-to-be, Lyndisty—*

Groaning, Vir dropped the document as if it were alive and trying to bite him. It went on, of course, about Lyndisty's parents, and about the wonderful entertainments that were being prepared, the fifteen-course meal that would be served, the performers from seven worlds who would exhibit their talents, the two hundred Narn slaves who would be pressed into service for the occasion, the redecorating of the residence that was now under way, the private transportation that would be provided to all guests, the brands of alcohol that would be imported at great expense—along with a famous bartender, the great Geesh, who did not come cheap. In fact, it went on for hundreds of words about the greatness of this upcoming event—the event of the year on Centauri Prime, no doubt—and about all the media coverage it would receive, the heads of state who would no doubt attend, the celebrities, the important, and those who had to be seen at the finest gatherings. In fact, according to the document, this would perhaps be the finest gathering *ever* on Centauri Prime, all in Vir Cotto's honor!

Well, not exactly . . .

Vir groaned again, pushing the offending document farther away from him; he pushed it with the heel of his boot until it once again resided beneath the chair from which he had so recently retrieved it.

For he knew that though that piece of paper bedecked in ribbons and frills and expensive seals invited him to a fete in his own honor, what it really invited him to was a trap that would destroy the rest of his life, with the announcement of the one thing he dreaded most: the wedding date.

CHAPTER 21

IF Michael Garibaldi was good at nothing else (which was not true), he was certainly good at getting (i.e., smuggling) items (in this case, three officers from Babylon 5, disguised as three Centauri) from the place they were to the place they needed to be.

Susan Ivanova was amazed at the ease with which she and her two companions found themselves on Centauri Prime. Most of the short trip had been spent in going over their identities as jewelry traders and in trying to solidify their individual characters; the only part she was still rusty on was the jewelry business itself—she had trouble telling a Narnian ruby from an Earth garnet, but there was always the portable scanner she had programmed for mineral identification to help her.

Obviously her two companions were not worried: Garibaldi slept while the ship docked, and Franklin looked almost bored.

"Aren't you worried at all, Stephen?" Ivanova asked, curious.

"Are you?" he countered, taking his eyes from the window he had been peering out.

"Worried? Not much. Anxious, maybe. Like just before a battle. There's a job to do and I'm getting myself ready to do it."

Franklin nodded. "That's the way I get ready for triage, too." He turned to regard Garibaldi. "Our security chief, on the other hand . . ."

Ivanova smiled, instantly wondering how she looked in her Centauri makeup. "I think Garibaldi is looking on this as one big sleep period."

Seemingly asleep, Garibaldi said, "Just trying to act like James Bond. Nothing bothered the guy."

Ivanova shook her head. "I tried reading one of the books. It was too much like little boys playing for my tastes. Bond has his toys—and the way he treats women!"

Garibaldi grinned with his eyes still closed and said, "That was my favorite thing about the books!"

Ivanova rolled her eyes. "I'm not surprised."

Garibaldi, still smiling, opened his eyes and stretched. "Just joking, of course," he said, and winked at Franklin, who grinned. Becoming serious, Garibaldi said, "We in yet?"

Franklin looked out the window. "Just about docked, Michael. I can't wait to have a look at the local life-forms."

"Oh, you'll get plenty of that," Garibaldi assured him.

Ivanova, suddenly serious, said, "It's time for you to take charge of this mission, Michael."

Garibaldi groaned. "You know I don't feel comfortable with that—"

"We've been over this before. It's my decision, and I think it's vital. Once we get to Centauri Prime, a woman in charge would raise more than a few eyebrows. It might even get us caught. And anyway, you have more experience in these special-ops things. Believe me, I'll take charge when I think I should."

Garibaldi sighed. "If that's the way you want it. And are you sure we shouldn't try to get in touch with Vir after we land?"

Ivanova shook her head. "Captain Sheridan and I considered and then rejected it. It would put *him* in too much danger. We're on our own on this."

Garibaldi consented, "All right. Then I think it's time we start referring to each other in our Centauri personas. Right, Mita?"

Her alias was Mita Cornova. Garibaldi's was Pir Chetski, and Franklin's was Jato Mindara. "Right, Pir," Ivanova countered.

Garibaldi laughed and said, "That's Mr. Chetski to you." He turned to the doctor. "And you, Mr. Mindara? Have you been in the jewelry business long?"

Franklin said, "Exactly two days."

Garibaldi held up a finger. "Remember what I said: stay in character!"

Franklin nodded and said, "Been in the jewelry business all my life. In fact, emeralds *are* my life."

"Very good, Jato."

"Whatever you say, Pir."

"Actually, we were damned lucky to get the gems to peddle," Ivanova said. Trying to act in character, she said, "Isn't that right, Pir?"

Garibaldi shrugged and smiled. "It helps to have confiscated goods. Our little hoard was due to go back to Earth just before we broke away. The fact that gems seem to be more valuable here doesn't hurt, either." Just as they felt the bump of the ship's hard dock, he added, "And I must say, Ms. Cornova, that shaved head of yours looks lovely."

Without missing a beat, Ivanova chimed in, "And I can't tell you how much I admire that peacock sitting on *your* head."

There was a hiss of the air locks being opened, as the three of them looked at one another and laughed.

CHAPTER 22

G'KAR's new cell was even dirtier than the last one.
It was small, with a lower ceiling that, the Narn
noted, made it easy for Londo to tower over him. He
lay on a cot against one wall, which was little more
than a flat board covered with a long rag.

"If we hadn't moved you, everything would be
lost by now," Londo reported.

"True," G'Kar answered, a slight smile on his
lips.

"Are you grinning perhaps because your cutthroat assassins murdered five of my men?"

"The thought has passed through my mind—and I
must admit it gives me pleasure when it does."

Londo brought his face close to the Narn's. "You
try my patience, G'Kar. If we did not need one another—"

"We would probably both be dead at this moment," G'Kar pointed out. "I would have killed you
the first time you walked into my cell—and then I, of
course, would have been killed by whatever guards
were nearby. But I at least would have died happy."

"And now your happiness depends on me!"

"That is the biggest irony of all. And *your* happiness depends on *me*."

"Yes!"

G'Kar managed a laugh. "It is a strange universe sometimes, is it not, Mollari?"

"Strange, yes. And cruel, too."

"Oh, yes," G'Kar said, suddenly remembering his most recent episode with Cartagia's pain technicians.

"But I ask you now: Do you have any idea where these Narns might be now?"

"I would tell you to still look underground. That is where they will stay, because that is where they will be most safe."

"Their safety doesn't concern me anymore."

"I told you, Mollari, that if they are harmed—"

Londo's face twisted into a hard sneer. "And I tell you now that if they are caught, they will be killed. Now that they have spilled Centauri blood, it would look more than suspicious if they were not dealt with when they were captured. As it is, I can spare only so many of my loyal men to search for them, and now that five of those men have been slaughtered—"

"I will not break my word; their safety must be provided for—"

"Yes, you will break your word! Because this is your choice, G'Kar. I give you the lives of those Narn soldiers against the freedom of your homeworld. If the assassins are caught, they must be killed; if they are not, our plans may be exposed. Make your choice, G'Kar."

Realizing that Londo was dead serious, G'Kar

understood with a sinking heart that he had no other choice. "You make things very difficult, Mollari."

"Life is difficult, G'Kar."

Bowing his head, G'Kar said, "Then I agree."

"Good," Mollari said, and immediately left the room.

As the door clanged shut, G'Kar, feeling an even greater weight than he had so recently borne drop upon his shoulders, said a silent prayer, and asked the forgiveness of the few in their sacrifice for the many.

CHAPTER 23

L'KAN kept his men moving.

He knew now that time was not on their side. Already they had avoided two Centauri patrols; there would be more.

In their favor, though, was the fact that the workday had once more resumed, and there were plenty of mining crews and tunneling crews to hide among. Below ground the Centauri slave masters seemed more lax than above ground; in many cases, they seemed content to while away their day by reading or sleeping, leaving most of the supervision to the Narns themselves. L'Kan had discovered that this was not the madness it seemed, since any escaping Narn was quickly caught and dealt with. L'Kan concluded from the relatively small patrols that seemed to be hunting them that someone on Centauri wanted them dealt with—but dealt with quietly.

Which was something to ponder—and make use of, if possible.

So hiding had not been a problem, though completing their mission had. Another nocturnal foray into the prison by Ra'Nik alone had proved futile. G'Kar's new cell was nowhere to be found.

So perhaps it was time to change the mission.

Perhaps it was time to do something . . . different.

CHAPTER 24

"I FEEL SO . . . silly!" Vir said.

"Nonsense," Londo Mollari countered, "this is a perfectly good way for you to get out of your so-called death trap."

"It *is* a death trap, Londo! If I go to that gala, Lyndisty will have my head on a silver platter!"

Londo snapped, "Then do what I say, Vir! And hold still!"

Suspended upside down, Vir tried not to squirm as Londo applied the last of his ministrations: on Vir's face were now ten large mushroom-shaped appendages.

Mollari held a mirror before Vir's face, and Vir screamed. "I look *horrible*!"

"You're *supposed* to look horrible, Vir! These are Trivorian face leeches we're talking about!"

"But do they have to look so . . ." Vir waved his hands as if he were pushing something away. "So . . . blech?"

"Yes! They do!"

Londo slowly lowered Vir from his perch. When

he stood, Vir saw that the leeches stayed in the curled-up position Londo had arranged them in.

"Stop looking in the mirror, Vir! If they were real, you would be writhing in pain right now!"

"But they . . . *look* so real!"

"Yes, they do. They were very useful to me on two occasions." A smile of satisfied remembrance came onto Londo's face. "The wife in question ran from me as if I were on fire!" He turned a baleful eye on Vir. "But you will sit still—or I will pull them off your face and leave immediately!"

"All right!" Vir cried, in a panic. "I won't move!"

"Good! Then call this woman, and get her to leave you alone!" At the door, Londo turned. "And be sure to be upside down when you talk to her! It's supposed to be the only way to keep from dying with these things on your face!"

When Londo had left, Vir checked his appearance once more in the mirror, winced at the sight, positioned himself upside down in front of the communications screen by draping himself over the back of a chair, and then brought Lyndisty's face up into view.

"Vir! What's happened to you!"

Vir moaned, and tried not to scratch, since the false leeches had all of a sudden become very itchy.

"I've . . . been afflicted, Lyndisty! Trivorian face leeches!"

"Poor Vir!"

"And they're *very* contagious! Which means we'd better not see one another for a while!"

"But who will take care of you, Vir?"

"I'll manage," Vir assured her earnestly. He moaned again, louder, as if in pain. "Even the doctors aren't supposed to come close, but they say I *may* pull through!"

On the screen, Lyndisty was doing something odd: her eyes downcast, she was checking a data screen, the edge of which Vir could barely see.

"Lyndisty, what are you doing?" Vir asked, trying to hide his alarm while at the same time scratching at a particularly insistent itch while Lyndisty was not watching.

She held up a finger. "Just wait, my dear. I'm checking something . . . yes!"

"What is it?" Vir demanded, alarmed at her cry of excitement.

"It says here, in our genetic code data, that my family is immune to Trivorian face leeches!" Her face brightened. "Which means that I can come and minister to you, Vir!"

"No!"

"What do you mean?" she asked in alarm. "Don't you want me to?"

"It's not that! It's just that . . . the code data may be wrong! Then you would have these horrible things on your face just like me! And they would suck your brains out through your skin, and kill you!"

She was smiling, checking something off-screen again. "Even better news, Vir!"

"Now what?" Vir moaned.

"It says that *your* genetic code is susceptible to only a mild case! The leeches should drop off by the time of my parents' gala!"

"Where did you get my genetic code data from, Lyndisty?" Vir turned pale.

"Don't be silly!" she answered with a laugh. "When our marriage was arranged, our families exchanged that data. It's common knowledge!"

"Right," Vir muttered. Already knowing he had lost this battle, and probably the war, Vir indulged in scratching viciously at one of the leeches, which promptly fell off.

"Oh, look," Vir said, with no animation. "One of them has already left my face. I guess I'm on the way to a cure."

"That's wonderful, Vir! Which means we'll see you at the gala!"

"Yes, I suppose you will . . ." Vir said tonelessly.

With a happy salutation, Lyndisty signed off.

Vir Cotto slid, defeated, down onto the chair seat and then continued to collapse off the chair to the floor, where he lay on his back, miserable, staring at the ceiling, thinking of what his head would look like on a silver platter.

CHAPTER 25

NIGHTFALL on Centauri Prime.
Michael Garibaldi, jewel merchant, turned to his two companions.

"Ready?" he asked.

"Ready as we'll ever be," Ivanova said.

Beside her, Franklin nodded. "Why not?" he said. "It's about time we did something other than talk about precious stones."

They had spent the day selling select stones at incredibly good prices to Centauri imperial guards, trying to find out what they needed to know. Finally, Ivanova had learned, from a particularly lascivious guard, who kept making lewd comments in between negotiations over the price of a certain ruby, that there had been an attempt to rescue G'Kar, that it had apparently failed, but that the Narns responsible were still at large.

"Don't worry, though," the guard had said, eyeing Ivanova's bald head as if he wanted to eat it for breakfast. "They'll be found soon and flogged to death."

"Speaking of flogging," Ivanova said, wanting

more than anything to kick this creature where it would most hurt him, but instead smiling pleasantly, "I've heard that the Narn G'Kar has been flogged repeatedly."

"Every day, and twice tomorrow!" The guard laughed. "Emperor Cartagia fancies this G'Kar as his play toy. I imagine one day soon the emperor will go too far with his electro-whip and . . ." The guard shrugged, leaving the rest to Susan's imagination.

She continued to smile pleasantly, holding up her jewel for his closer inspection.

"I'm still thinking," he said, continuing to stare at her head.

"Where do they keep this terrible Narn?" Ivanova asked innocently.

"Oh, he's closer than ever to the emperor now," the guard said.

"And just how close to the emperor would that be?" Susan asked.

"Oh, he's temporarily moved the Narn right into the palace, until they can find a new, more secure cell! This way Cartagia can have him tortured at a moment's notice!"

"I'd love to see this G'Kar," Ivanova ventured, trying not to gag as she tried to sound coquettish.

The guard said, "Eh?" and then, finally, took his eyes away from her head. "Not allowed," he said, gruffly. "How much for the ruby?" he asked, and Susan, smiling but wanting to scream, sold it to him for half what it was worth, just to get rid of him.

* * *

And here they were at night, trying to break into the palace itself.

There was a certain amount of commerce that went on in front of the palace, by the sparkling waters of the artificial lake with fountains that fronted the building; there was even more intimate business that went on at the top of the steps; and then there was more intimate business still that went on in the recesses of the building.

It was a stroke of incredible luck that one of the first Centauri they approached with their wares was a minister, a close adviser of Emperor Cartagia himself. The man was so impressed with their collection and their prices that he immediately ushered them inside the palace.

"There's no need to broadcast this good fortune you bring to anyone else," he said with an oily smile.

They immediately sold him three emeralds and a diamond that made his eyes widen.

"And where did you say you got these wonderful specimens, Mr. Chetski?" he asked.

"We didn't," Garibaldi said with a flash of his eyebrows.

"Ah . . ." The man was enraptured, looking over yet another emerald. "And these prices—how do you do it?"

"Volume," Garibaldi replied.

The other laughed. "Oh, you must come with me immediately and see the emperor."

"Now?" Ivanova said, startled by their good fortune.

"Of course! He is . . . entertaining, but he always has time for a good bargain!"

Trading glances, the three jewel merchants followed.

And there in one of the palace's lavish audience rooms Emperor Cartagia lounged on a red throne—and there, all but passed out on the floor of the chamber, lay G'Kar.

Garibaldi gritted his teeth. He saw that the others were doing their best to hide their reactions.

"A little more hot oil on his head, please!" the emperor said, raising a finger.

A guard approached G'Kar and tilted a steaming pot until a thin, nearly burning line of something blue and viscous dripped out.

A few drops hit the supine Narn, and he reared back his head and hissed in pain.

Garibaldi noted that there were burn marks all around G'Kar's head. He seemed insensible of where he was, and was beyond even trying to get up.

"What have we here?" Cartagia said, as the minister bid the three jewel merchants to approach.

As they had been instructed for such an occasion, the three paid their homage, and stood, eyes downcast.

"We wait on the emperor's pleasure," Garibaldi announced.

"Jewels?" Cartagia said brightly, after the minister had whispered in his ear.

"Look up at me, and come closer!" Cartagia ordered.

The three obeyed.

"Let me see what you have!" He turned to his minister. "And let me see what you have already purchased—which are probably the best of the lot!"

The minister's smile collapsed, and in resignation he drew out his pouch with his recent purchases.

All of the jewels present were laid out for the emperor's inspection.

"Lovely!" he said, choosing a handful.

G'Kar moaned, and the emperor, distracted, said to the nearest imperial guard, "Oh, take him to his room. You may kick him once when you get there."

The guard instantly obeyed and, with help, dragged G'Kar off.

As the emperor studied the jewels before him, Garibaldi followed the guards with his eyes, noting what corridor G'Kar was taken down. There was a door on the right that the guards opened, then dragged the Narn through.

"I'll take all of these! And do you have more?"

"Oh, yes," Ivanova said. She noted with some alarm that the emperor himself seemed to be staring at her bald head. *I hate bald,* she said to herself, making a mental note.

"We have . . . much more," Franklin declared, bowing.

"Good!" the emperor said. "Then you will return tomorrow night with your whole stock!"

"Of course, Emperor!" Garibaldi assured him, his attention back on the business at hand.

"And how much do you want for these?" Cartagia asked, indicating his choices.

They told him, and the emperor's eyes widened. "Such good prices!"

"Volume," Garibaldi explained.

Outside the palace, before the gently lapping waters of the artificial lake, Garibaldi admitted, "I can't believe our luck. Even James Bond didn't have luck like this."

"We should have no trouble getting to G'Kar tomorrow night," Ivanova speculated.

"And then we can get off this planet, and I can get out of these Centauri clothes!" Franklin complained.

"Now, now," Garibaldi said. "Until this is over, you're still Jato. Jato never complains like Stephen Franklin does."

Franklin's eyes narrowed. "Right."

"I did want to kick Cartagia in the face," Garibaldi said, "seeing what he's done to G'Kar."

Ivanova nodded. "Me, too."

"But how will we get G'Kar out?" Franklin asked.

"We'll need a diversion," Garibaldi said. He studied Ivanova for a moment and smiled mischievously. "I noticed Cartagia studying your head, sort of the way that guard did this afternoon—"

"No way," Susan protested. "I'd rather put on a clown wig than flirt with that reptile."

"You disappoint me, Mita," Garibaldi said. "Any jewel trader would jump at the chance of having a mad emperor stare at her head!" Quickly he added, "Actually, I've got a much better plan."

* * *

Within the palace, Emperor Cartagia called his sulking minister to his side.

"I know you kept at least three good specimens for yourself and didn't show them to me."

As the other blanched, the emperor waved off his agitation. "No matter. Keep them. But I want you to check on those jewelers."

"Emperor?"

Cartagia narrowed his eyes. "They seemed too good to be true. And, as we know, when something is too good to be true, it often is."

CHAPTER 26

ON Babylon 5, Sheridan turned from his communications screen as Delenn entered his office.

"You just missed a message from Garibaldi," he said brightly. "It seems they have a shot at rescuing G'Kar tomorrow."

"That's wonderful news, John," Delenn responded.

Sheridan grinned. "He even called me 'M' in the message. I *do* wish we could have gone with them."

"This 'cloak and dagger' appeals to you?" Delenn asked.

"Actually I prefer straight-out conflict. But when cloak and dagger is the way to get something done, I'm all for it."

"Then perhaps you can explain something to me," Delenn said. She wore the puzzled look she often did when wrestling with the vagaries of the English language. "If on your world you are to be a spy, must you wear a cloak and carry a dagger?"

Sheridan laughed. "No, no! It's just that . . ." His words trailed off. "Never mind!" He laughed. "It's just one of those strange Earth terms!"

"One of many, I might add," Delenn said.

"Yes," Sheridan agreed, "one of many. And now the reason I called you here: since Zack seems to have the rioting under control in Chief Garibaldi's absence, and since the Shadow and Vorlon scare in the Euphrates sector turned out to be baseless, I thought you and I deserved to be involved in this 'cloak-and-dagger' business."

"Captain!" Delenn said. "Surely you do not suggest that you and I don cloaks and wear daggers, and . . ."

Sheridan was laughing. "No, Delenn! Nothing that extreme! But in talking with Zack this morning it came to my attention that there's a little problem on Babylon 5 that could be solved utilizing a bit of espionage. It's not a big deal, and we'd be right here if we were needed. Also, we'd get to spend some real time together, the first since everything that happened with Anna. And also, to tell you the truth—"

"You feel left out," Delenn offered, smiling knowingly. "Your friends got to play at being spies, when it was you all along who wanted to be this 'James Bond' fellow."

Sheridan's mouth hung open.

"Am I right, John?"

"Well . . . yes, you are!"

"Good!" Delenn said. "Then I concur! As of this moment, you will be like James Bond, and I will be . . ." Her face clouded.

Sheridan grinned. "Oh, I've got a name for you, too."

CHAPTER 27

In their new hiding spot, much better, deeper, and more secretive than the old one, L'Kan told the others of his new plan.

"The circumstances dictate that we change tactics," he said. "The main objective is still in sight—but the way to this goal must be changed."

"Then is that why we spent the last day and night searching for this spot?" Ra'Nik inquired.

L'Kan noted that he seemed pleased. "Yes," L'Kan said. "It is essential that we have a secure spot, one that is hidden and that can be guarded."

The others nodded, and Ra'Nik held up his *ka'toc*.

"This plan is good," Ra'Nik said, studying the blade. "And once more Centauri blood will be spilled!"

"Only now," L'Kan announced, "it will be the blood of a Centauri who most deserves to die!"

CHAPTER 28

Londo was tiring of Vir's panic attacks. So *what* if the plan with the Trivorian face leeches didn't work? There was always another plan! Why couldn't Vir understand such things? He was beginning to seriously doubt that Vir had any ability at all—except to go into a frenzy.

And over a *woman*! Not that Londo did not understand temporarily going insane over a woman—but when one woke up from the insanity there was always a way to get rid of the mistake!

Why didn't Vir come up with something on his own!

And here he was, Londo Mollari, in the middle of the night, prowling the streets like a common criminal, on his way to meet a man who could supply him with an imitation Drazi head-sucker—something that no genetic screening could save Vir from! Londo had to give Lyndisty her due: she was a resourceful young woman! But this new plot would definitely get Vir out of the gala to be held in his honor by Lyndisty's parents. Londo's own invitation had ar-

rived this afternoon: he had of course accepted at
once. It would have been impolitic not to do so,
since they were such popular people—and besides,
their liquor would be *excellent*. But now, thinking of
the excellence of that liquor, the vintages Lyndisty's
parents would have access to due to their exalted
position, Londo was suddenly not so sure that getting Vir out of his predicament was such a good idea
after all—

Here, suddenly, in the midst of these pleasant
thoughts, on this shadowy nighttime walkway,
Londo found himself surrounded by five shadowy
figures.

"Who are you! Get out of my way!" he demanded. In the gloom he could not make out their
faces.

"You are Londo Mollari?" one of them asked.
He was tall, and his voice did not sound Centauri.

"Yes I am! And if you know what's good
for you, you will get out of my way immediately!"

But then one of them stepped into the light—and
Londo felt a sudden pang of terror grip him as he
understood what sort of predicament *he* was suddenly in.

"Narns!" Londo shouted.

"Yes, Mollari, Narns," the one who had stepped
into the light said.

"Assassins!" Londo called out.

"The night is dark, and the streets are quiet, and
no one listens to you," the other threatened. The

others closed in around Londo, who shrunk away in fear.

"And," the Narn added, as his four companions laid hold of the Centauri, "perhaps assassins is not a bad word."

CHAPTER 29

THIS time it was Susan Ivanova who dreamed of G'Kar:

> A blasted planet that she knew at once to be Narn. She could almost see the ruined fertility—where once things had been lush, now they were burned: greens had turned to browns and rusted reds, blue water to scorched earth, blue sky to ash. In the distance she could see a burned city, but she found herself on a plain that looked like Mars in its worst times—a boulder-strewn, oxidized wasteland. Overhead, the dusty sky shone sickly red-yellow, and heat that would have felt good in another clime merely made the air feel close and baked.
>
> Ivanova was alone, but she felt watched. She looked down to see herself in her Babylon 5 uniform—but when she felt her face she found that her head was bald except for the Centauri ponytail. She had no water, and was thirsty; no food and felt hungry.
>
> She began to walk toward the distant city, but

found that no matter how far she walked, it seemed to recede into the distance away from her.

"This isn't getting me anywhere," she said.

Overhead she heard a whirring, and then saw a Narn ship approaching from the direction of the city. It grew in size and made a landing a kilometer or so ahead of her.

She walked toward it—but once again, the ship acted as the city had, and refused to grow closer.

"I've had just about enough of this," she said, frustrated.

A figure now stood next to the Narn craft. It was too distant to make out its features, but it looked familiar . . .

"G'Kar?" Susan called out.

The figure silently looked at her.

She called again, but the figure merely regarded her, then climbed back into its ship. In a moment the Narn craft lifted off and headed back toward the city.

"Now, that's weird," Susan said to herself— and then G'Kar's voice suddenly boomed in her ear, "Go home."

She woke up with a start. "That's one for the books," Ivanova said, sitting up in bed, shaking the dream from her eyes. It had seemed so *real*.

In her Centauri quarters, she lay down to sleep again—and once again had the same dream.

After the third time, she rose out of bed—convinced something was wrong—and went to wake up Garibaldi.

CHAPTER 30

Now Vir discovered what *real* panic was.

"Where can he *be*?" he fussed, worrying that Londo would never arrive and that he would be stuck, once and for all, with going to the gala Lyndisty's parents had planned for him. He knew that if Londo's next plan—something to do with a giant head-sucker; Londo hadn't been specific, just specific enough to alarm Vir—didn't work, then all was lost.

But where was Londo? He should have been in Vir's quarters long ago, and the night was wasting away . . .

Finally Vir called Londo's quarters—but he was not there.

Where could he be?

Beginning to feel true alarm, Vir dressed for outdoors and set out to find Londo. He started with the obvious spots—the Imperial Palace, the few watering holes where Londo had been seen drinking recently, a couple of gambling houses—but Londo was nowhere to be found. Finally, Vir tried Londo's residence—but, once again, found that he was not at home.

"What could have happened to him?" Vir asked, half out loud.

Before long, he had an answer.

A block from Londo's residence, someone stepped out of a side street and knocked Vir down. The figure then helped Vir to his feet but instead of apologizing pulled him into the side street, keeping an iron grip on Vir's arm.

"Don't speak and you won't die," the figure said, and with a barely concealed gasp Vir saw that the figure, a Narn, was holding an unsheathed Narn sword, a *ka'toc*. Vir knew what a *ka'toc* was—and knew that it couldn't be sheathed again until blood was spilled—

The Narn held the sword up for Vir's closer inspection.

"It's not for you—but it will be if you don't listen closely," the Narn hissed.

Vir squeaked, "Certainly!"

"Good. Your name is Vir Cotto?"

"Yes!"

"And you work for Londo Mollari?"

"Sort of," Vir said, beginning to qualify.

The iron grip tightened; the sword edge glinted in caught nightlight. "Yes or no?" the figure demanded.

"Yes!" Vir croaked.

"Then listen carefully, Vir Cotto. We have Londo Mollari, and we will not release him until G'Kar is set free. Do you understand that?"

"Yes, but—"

"But what?"

"I . . ."

Suddenly Vir's head was spinning; this Narn wanted G'Kar free, but the truth of it was that G'Kar did not want to be freed because he had made a bargain with Londo. And if Londo was killed, then the bargain would be negated. And . . .

Vir was suddenly dizzy.

"You have to let Londo go!" Vir blurted out. "And you can't free G'Kar!"

The blade came very close to Vir's face; the edge ticked his nose. "What did you say? Repeat it, and die on this street!"

"What I said was," Vir began, but then he hesitated.

"Yes?" the Narn asked.

"Ummm, never mind. Perhaps another time."

"The next time we meet you will die, unless you heed my warning. Free G'Kar, and perhaps Londo Mollari will live."

"Perhaps?" Vir said in a meek voice.

"Perhaps."

Then the Narn dropped Vir in a heap on the street, and was gone.

"Perhaps?" Vir repeated in a squeaky, very confused voice, this time to himself.

CHAPTER 31

"I'M telling you, Michael—"

Sitting up in bed, trying to keep awake as Ivanova paced nervously in front of him in his cramped quarters, Garibaldi held a finger up.

"Remember," he said. "While we're here, we're Centauri!"

"All right, then. I'm telling you, *Pir,* that there's something wrong with G'Kar's situation."

"You bet there is. He's being tortured every day by a madman—and we're going to do something about it." He cocked his head and considered a moment. "And now that I think about it, I think I like 'Mr. Chetski' better than just plain old 'Pir.' "

Ivanova snorted with frustration, and Garibaldi, running a hand through his false peacock's fringe of hair, said, "Look, all right, what if there is something wrong? How are we supposed to know? There are two groups trying to free G'Kar, and you're telling me neither of us should do it?"

Ivanova frowned. "I don't know *what* I mean. It's just a feeling that something is very wrong with what we're doing—"

"Should we leave?" Garibaldi interjected.

"No . . ."

"Then what should we do?"

Ivanova shook her head. "Sorry I woke you up, Garib—" She stopped, and smiled. "Sorry I woke you up, Mr. Chetski."

"Now you've got it right!" Garibaldi congratulated her. "And if you don't mind, I'd like to get back to sleep. We've got a big day tomorrow. Gonna sell some jewels to a madman. And free G'Kar." He looked at Susan. "Right?"

After a moment she nodded, though she was still frowning slightly.

"Right," she said finally.

But as she left Garibaldi's room, the nagging feeling wouldn't leave her . . .

CHAPTER 32

"This is all very mysterious, John," Delenn said, giving Sheridan her amused smile. She had met Sheridan where he asked, in a little-used area of Down Below that even looked faintly *dangerous*.

"And it's supposed to be!" the captain answered, and then he added, "And don't talk so loud! They might hear us!"

"Who is 'they'?" Delenn asked.

"The bad guys! Agents from SMALL!"

"What is . . . SMALL?" Delenn inquired, frowning.

"The Secret Martian Allies!"

Delenn's frown suddenly became concern. "Is there such a thing? It sounds . . . dangerous!"

Still smiling, which confused Delenn even more, Sheridan said, "It *is* dangerous! They could destroy us and everything we believe in! And no one but me knows about them!"

Now Delenn looked alarmed. "If this is so serious, you should not be smiling, John! And here is something you have kept from me, this . . . secret organization that even the Rangers don't know about—I must say that you had no right—''

Sheridan was laughing, even while he donned a trench coat and put on dark glasses.

"Delenn—I made it all up! It's just a game!''

Now Delenn looked vastly confused; even more so when the captain unrolled a bundle and handed *her* a trench coat and dark glasses to wear.

"Put them on!'' Sheridan urged.

"I still don't understand . . .''

"Look,'' Sheridan said, taking her by the shoulders and looking into her eyes. "After everything we've been through lately, I thought it was time that the two of us took a complete break. Since a real vacation is out of the question, the next best thing we could do is escape while we're still on Babylon 5. Remember I told you there was a little problem on the station that could be solved using a bit of espionage?''

"Yes,'' Delenn said. Some of her confusion had evaporated, but she still was not completely with him.

"Well, it has something to with Martian smuggling. It seems a little black-market operation has been running on Babylon 5 for a while, illegally bringing products from the nonaligned worlds through the station and then selling them on Mars. They avoid all the fees and taxes. The products are nothing dangerous, not drugs or weapons. Actually,'' he said, grinning, "they're toys. But the operation still needs to be shut down, and up until now Garibaldi and his men haven't been able to crack it using conventional means. So . . . you and I are going to be spies.''

He helped her don the trench coat and watched while she put on the glasses.

''Everything's . . . too dark!''

Sheridan chuckled and adjusted the light filter on the side of the glasses until she said, ''That's better!''

''So!'' Sheridan said. ''What do you think!''

Delenn looked at herself, and at Sheridan.

''I think we stick out like sore toes!''

''You mean 'sore thumbs,' don't you?''

''Whatever!'' She was smiling now. ''But this could be . . . fun!''

''That's the point!'' Sheridan agreed. ''Even adults need to play every once in a while. It lets the steam off, takes the mind off all the rotten things that happen day in and day out. This will be our vacation.'' He smiled warmly.

''I think I shall enjoy being a spy!''

He showed her his wrist, which still bore his link. ''If either of us is really needed, I've instructed C&C and Zack to get in touch with us. Otherwise, we won't be bothered.''

''Good!''

Sheridan announced, ''Then from this moment on, we are no longer Captain John Sheridan and Ambassador Delenn—but Agents X and Y!''

''Am I X or Y?''

''I think Y would be better,'' Sheridan said.

''I think I want to be . . . X!''

''X it is, then!'' Sheridan declared, and they both laughed.

CHAPTER 33

"I'M telling you fools, you're ruining *everything!*"
Hands tied behind him, sitting in an uncomfortable chair, Londo Mollari let outrage overrule his fear. If he could just make these Narns understand—

"And I've told you, *Ambassador,* that there is a very good chance that you will die when all of this is over."

L'Kan regarded his prisoner with what he hoped looked like complete contempt.

"Kill me now! It will make no difference then!" Londo sputtered.

"And you mean for me to believe that I must let you go, and let G'Kar continue to be tortured—all for the betterment of my homeworld?"

"I *know* it sounds ridiculous, but you must believe me!" With effort, Londo tried to calm himself. His backside was increasingly uncomfortable on this so-called chair he had been trussed to.

"Do you by any chance have a pillow?" he asked, lowering his voice to ambassadorial reasonableness.

"We should have staked you to the floor," Ra'Nik chimed in, wanting to spit. "If it weren't for your trade value, you would be very uncomfortable indeed by now."

"Will you please *listen* to me!" Londo pleaded. "As I've told you, G'Kar and I have an agreement! At the end of which, the Narn homeworld will be freed! You have my pledge on that!"

"And your pledge is worth nothing," L'Kan said. For perhaps the twentieth time since they had arrived in this hiding spot, the Narn commander leader brought his unsheathed *ka'toc* close to the ambassador's face.

"If you mean to give me a shave, then do it— otherwise, take that thing away from me!" Londo said impatiently.

The blade came more than close—suddenly there was a thin gash across the Centauri's cheek.

"You've cut me!"

"Yes, I have," L'Kan said. He examined his *ka'toc,* then, satisfied, sheathed it.

This time he brought his face, instead of his sword, close to Londo. "The next time I draw my *ka'toc,*" he spat, "I will thrust it into your innards."

"I've told you—" Londo began again.

A blow from the back of L'Kan's hand silenced his words and drove him down into unconsciousness.

CHAPTER 34

WHAT will I do? What will I do?

Vir Cotto paced his quarters like a caged beast. It seemed that his whole world had been turned upside down in a matter of days.

First, Lyndisty had come back into his life, all but trapping him into marriage.

And now—Londo kidnapped!

What will I do?

Actually, he had no idea what he would do. What he *wanted* to do was take the next available ship back to Babylon 5 and hide in his quarters there. Perhaps he would even move to Down Below and live with the Lurkers for a while.

Perhaps he would *become* a lurker, dress in shabby clothes, steal food, trade with other thieves, and fight for his life daily—anything would be preferable to this!

"What am I going to do!" he cried out loud.

There was no answer from the room, and he continued to pace.

Got to think, got to think, he thought.

But think of what? In two days his life would be

over anyway, when Lyndisty's ''gala'' brought him
to the gallows. So what did it matter if Londo was
gone? What good had Londo ever done him, anyway? All Londo did was look out for himself, and
plot, and scheme, and then look out for himself
some more. So what if Narns had kidnapped him?
Let him scheme with the Narns for a change. Vir
had no doubt that Londo would be leading the Narn
commandos, given a little time and a lot of talking.
Londo could talk the paint off a wall.

Are you crazy? he thought. Of *course* Londo
would not be able to negotiate with the Narns. They
hated him! They would probably kill him anyway,
even if they did manage to get G'Kar freed.

Which could not happen, of course, because then
the Narn homeworld would never be released from
bondage.

And then there *was* the fact that he, Vir, unac-
countably, unjustifiably, actually *liked* Londo . . .

The Narns had to be convinced to let Londo go!
But how can I do that?

His thoughts were so jumbled: Lyndisty, Londo;
Londo, Lyndisty—

I'll have to free Londo myself!

That was it! That was it!

But how?

*Perhaps I'll get killed in the attempt—and then all
my problems will be solved!*

If I'm dead, I won't have to marry Lyndisty!

For a moment, that possibility actually looked at-
tractive, and Vir stood with a finger in the air,
pondering it—

What are you doing!

He began to pace, and pace, and pace.

There had to be a better way, a saner way—one that kept him alive and solved *all* of his problems . . .

CHAPTER 35

"READY?" Garibaldi asked.

"Ready." Franklin nodded, rolling the last of his gems up in flannel. "And didn't you say the same thing the last time?"

"Habit," Michael said. He turned to Ivanova. "And you?"

"Ready as I'll ever be," she replied.

Garibaldi gave a mock frown. "Don't tell me that—now I know we're in trouble."

As they left Garibaldi's quarters on their way to their meeting with the emperor, Susan said, "Have I told you that your sense of humor, Pir, is a lot like someone else's I know, a guy named Garibaldi?"

"Sounds like a great guy."

"Not at all," she said. "His sense of humor is terrible."

When they arrived at the imperial palace, they noted a few more imperial guards around than on their previous visit.

"You getting a bad feeling about this?" Garibaldi wondered aloud.

Ivanova nodded. "Very bad. I think if we walk into the palace we don't walk out."

"I say we go back to our quarters and think about this a little. We can always come back later."

"Agreed," she said, and Franklin also assented.

When they entered Garibaldi's quarters there was nothing amiss. But as soon as the door was closed there came a knock.

"You call for room service?" Ivanova asked, not laughing.

Garibaldi drew the PPG handgun hidden in his boot and said, emphatically, "No."

He nodded toward the other room. "Why don't you two wait in there?"

Ivanova and Franklin withdrew to the adjoining room. In a moment there came sounds of a scuffle and they were driven back out, hands over their heads. As Garibaldi turned his attention to them the door flew open and two heavily armed imperial guards rushed into the room. One of them drove the barrel of his PPG rifle at Garibaldi's wrist, causing him to drop his own weapon.

The imperial guard motioned with his rifle for Garibaldi to raise his hands.

Behind Ivanova and Franklin were two more guards, who had obviously been hidden in the adjoining room.

"May I ask—" Garibaldi demanded, trying to sound outraged.

"All your questions will be answered," echoed a familiar voice from the doorway—and into the room, smiling, came the emperor's minister they had met the day before.

CHAPTER 36

DELENN giggled. "I can't help it," she said. "I feel silly."

Sheridan frowned. "I told you, X, that you have to take this in the right spirit. If you don't take it at least a *little* seriously, then we'll get nothing out of it at all!"

Delenn could see the captain not thirty paces away, hiding behind a column. Yet she had to hide here, behind a pile of old boxes somewhere in the depths of Down Below, and pretend that she and the captain were in mortal danger.

"But we're hunting *toys*!" She giggled into the special link she had been given; it was set to a frequency that only she and John could use.

"We're hunting spies!" the captain shot back, a little annoyed. "And from what we know, their contraband is somewhere in this area. And they're members of SMALL!"

Delenn was laughing uncontrollably now. "Ah, yes, the infamous SMALL. The Secret Martian Allies! I—" She broke off in a fit of giggling.

"Then I'll go on alone," the captain said, a little peevishly.

"Oh, John," Delenn cajoled, meaning to calm him down, but when she looked he was gone.

She spoke into her link, but he would not answer.

"Very well, then," she said, folding her arms. "If you do not want me to 'play,' I will not play. I will wait right here for this charade to be over."

She counted to ten, then ten again, and, still with her arms folded across her trench coat, she refused to call him.

After a further count, she did try again, saying, "John, I think this silliness has gone far enough, don't you?"

There was no answer.

"John? Would you please talk to me?"

Still, her link remained silent.

She looked out of her hiding spot—where the captain had been there was now another figure, clad in dark red, with a cap pulled low over his brow.

Delenn almost called out, but the figure was acting very suspiciously, digging through a stack of boxes near where the captain had been. He pushed a couple of cartons aside, then examined a particular one and tore it open. He rooted around inside, then pulled something from within the carton, hid it in his clothing, and moved off.

After a few moments, Delenn tried her link again.

"John? I just saw something very odd!"

Still there was no answer.

Cautiously, Delenn moved out of her hiding spot. With further caution, she moved to where the captain, and then the red-clad figure, had been.

She knelt down to examine the discarded box the mysterious figure had been digging through.

She opened it and discovered a mass of extremely light, large balls. She lifted one out, and as she held it between her palms and pressed it, it disintegrated with a pop, letting out a puff of air.

"How charming!" she said.

She dug deeper into the box. There was wrapping within and, trapped inside the wrapping, what appeared to be a doll's arm, which had obviously been torn loose.

"Toys . . ." Delenn murmured to herself, with a mixture of curiosity and amusement.

Something caught her eye, a glint where the arm had been torn from the rest of the doll.

Carefully, using her thumb and index finger, she tweezered out a tiny chip. Holding it up for examination in the dim light, she examined it further.

It appeared to be a tiny electronic component, similar to others she had seen.

Similar to one in particular.

She had seen this sort of thing before, during the Earth-Minbari war, when those on the Grey Council had been well versed in the methods of Earth warfare, and weaponry.

The chip she held was a detonator used for only one thing—

Weapons.

Very large weapons.

CHAPTER 37

"I⊤ is very odd," L'Kan said, "that hours have gone by, and we have heard nothing from Vir Cotto about arrangements for your exchange for G'Kar."

Londo, whose backside was as sore as it had ever been in his life, had nearly given up trying to explain.

After all, they were *Narns*—and what did Narns know, anyway?

Wearily, he looked up at his captor.

"As I've explained to you a hundred times, Vir cannot and will not make such an arrangement! He knows what is at stake!"

"The only thing at stake is your miserable life, Mollari. The rest is all lies."

"Then believe what you will," Londo said with finality. He grimaced in pain. "But can you find it in your soulless heart to get me a pillow!"

Outside the secret place where L'Kan held his prisoner, the four other Narn commandos led by Ra'Nik waited for Vir Cotto to return to his quarters. He had been gone for an hour, and the Narns assumed that he was off making arrangements for the transfer of the two prisoners.

But when Vir returned, he had *shopping packages* in his hands!

The four Narns rushed upon him as he entered his quarters, and fairly pushed him spinning into the front room.

"What are you doing!" Vir blustered, trying to keep hold of his purchases. With some difficulty, as he was being thrown into the nearest chair, he managed to toss the bundles onto another chair in passing.

"When will G'Kar be freed?" Ra'Nik demanded.

"You!" Vir exclaimed, recognizing the Narn who had accosted him the night before.

"Yes, me! And do you remember *this,* also?"

Ra'Nik showed Vir his *ka'toc*.

Wincing, Vir admitted, "Very well, thank you."

"What are the arrangements?" Ra'Nik demanded.

"Well, actually," Vir began, "I haven't made any yet. These things take time . . ."

"Time is something you don't have!" the Narn growled, advancing on him.

Vir drew himself up and, summoning his courage, said, "Would you . . . believe me if I said that it would be better if G'Kar remains where he is?"

"You mean tortured?" The Narn's anger flared. "And treated like a dog?"

"Well, not that part, exactly. But if G'Kar stays where he is, and you let Londo go, there's a good chance that your homeworld will be freed." Vir tried to smile. "Would you believe that, by any chance?"

Ra'Nik snorted, and turned to his companions.

"He spouts the same nonsense as Mollari!"

One of the others proposed, "Let's kill him now."

Frightened, Vir stammered, "That . . . wouldn't be a good idea . . ."

One of the Narns was rifling through Vir's packages.

"Umm," Vir squeaked, pointing meekly. "Do you mind? Some of that is very expensive . . ."

With a roar the Narn knocked the packages over. With a sinking heart, Vir heard something break inside one of them.

"Listen, Vir Cotto," Ra'Nik ordered, as his companions continued to destroy Vir's purchases. "Listen well to what I say. You will have two more days to arrange the release of G'Kar. If you do not do that, then the criminal Londo Mollari will be executed, and for good measure, we will return here and kill you also."

Brandishing his *ka'toc,* Ra'Nik turned and motioned for the others to leave.

After they had gone, Vir rose gingerly and went to where his recently purchased packages lay scattered and trampled on the floor. He picked up one in particular; within, there was the tinkle of broken glass.

And Lyndisty would have liked it, too. Perhaps to

*the point where she would have put the wedding off
for a while* . . .

Moaning, Vir sat down in the jumble of broken
trinkets, put his head in his hands, and wondered for
the hundredth time that day, *What am I going to do?*

CHAPTER 38

"It has come to my attention," the emperor's minister said, "that there may be certain . . . irregularities in the way you have conducted business."

"Irregularities?" Garibaldi echoed innocently, as he and his two companions sat, at gunpoint, on Garibaldi's bed.

The adviser smiled. "Yes. There are, it seems, certain local . . . *permits* that have not been properly attended to, and certain other . . . *procedures* that haven't been properly, shall we say, followed."

Ivanova leaned over and whispered into Garibaldi's ear, "He's looking for a bribe!"

Michael said, "Ah! Of course! And what, exactly, would those permits and . . . procedures consist of?"

The minister motioned for the imperial guards to leave. One by one, they trailed out and closed the door behind them.

Franklin asked, "Is the emperor's minister perhaps . . . shall we say, disappointed that some of his fine purchases yesterday were . . . shall we say, *transferred* to the emperor's possession?"

The minister nearly laughed. "I, my friend, would not be so bold to say such a thing. But let us just leave it at the fact that I would appreciate a . . . *preview* of what is to be shown to the emperor." He held up a hand. "And you needn't worry about being late for your appointment. I changed it to this evening in advance. So we have . . . plenty of time for a preview. I"—again he smiled—"wouldn't want the emperor to be shown shoddy goods, would I?"

Garibaldi smiled to himself and said, "So you're here to make sure that anything unworthy of the emperor's attention is skimmed off—I mean, *removed* from review before it can offend his eyes. Am I right?"

The emperor's minister bowed slightly. "More than correct. Shall we proceed?"

The minister nearly drooled as they brought out their finest specimens and began to lay them out on velvet before him.

"And so," the emperor's minister said much later, "let us just say that this little . . . arrangement will go unspoken of, shall we?"

Garibaldi bowed his head. "Of course."

Rolling up the last of his treasure in flannel cloth and putting it into his pocket, the emperor's minister turned to leave.

"Until tonight, then," he said.

"Until tonight," Garibaldi confirmed. "And may I ask you something?"

The minister turned and smiled. "After the excellent bargains you have just given me, please ask anything!''

Garibaldi tried to sound nonchalant. ''Who was that Narn we saw yesterday in the emperor's presence?''

A look of distaste crossed the minister's face. ''His name is G'Kar. Why would you even ask?''

''Would it be possible for us to . . . examine him when we come to see the emperor tonight?''

The minister looked surprised. ''Why would you possibly want to do that?''

''It's . . . said that Narns, especially of the higher rank, have a facility with certain gems, and are able to discern the really fine differences in quality in semiprecious stones such as opals.''

The minister considered for a moment, then ventured, ''And if this Narn were able to discern these differences, you would be able to separate the truly fine stones from the rest?''

''Of course!'' Garibaldi guaranteed.

''I'll see what can be done,'' the minister said. And before he could say it himself, Michael interrupted:

''And we would, of course, feel compelled to provide you with some of these finest specimens . . . for your trouble.''

''Until tonight, then,'' the minister said, and left.

As soon as they were alone, Ivanova turned to Garibaldi. ''Narns as semiprecious stone graders?'' She shook her head in wonder.

''How's that for quick thinking?'' he said, grinning.

''Now all we have to do,'' Franklin said, ''is

figure out a way to get G'Kar out of the cell, out of the imperial palace, and off Centauri Prime.''

Susan said, ''Hope we brought some opals . . .''

CHAPTER 39

CAPTAIN Sheridan was mildly peeved that Delenn was gone.

He knew she thought this game they were playing was silly. But that was part of the point: to relax. Here he was, back where they had started, and she was nowhere to be found.

He had to assume she had given up and gone back to her quarters. He wished he could be sure, but the link he had specially programmed had gone on the blink and he hadn't been able to use it for anything; even after reconfiguring it for normal use he had been unable to get in touch with Zack and finally had just given up.

But he *had* expected to find Delenn here where he had left her—and now she was gone.

What would James Bond do?

Go on, of course!

One thing he *did* have to admit, though, was that he felt pretty silly in this trench coat and dark glasses.

No matter—since he wore something even more appropriate underneath.

He removed the trench coat, rolled it up after stowing the dark glasses in one of the pockets, and stashed it between two large cartons.

"Now, *this* is more like James Bond!" he said, smoothing the black turtleneck down over the black jeans he wore; on his feet were black boots, completing the outfit.

At that moment he heard a sound. He looked up, almost saying, "Delenn?" but held his tongue.

It was not Delenn, but a furtive, short figure wearing a blue hat, who began to rummage in a box about ten meters away.

Sheridan pulled back out of sight and watched.

The short man found a particular box, opened it, pulled something out, then closed the box and put it back where it had been.

Sheridan waited for the man to move off, then approached the box and pulled it out and opened it.

It was filled with dolls!

Toys!

Then the tip they'd had about this being the area where the smuggled toys were being stored had been correct.

Removing one of the dolls, Sheridan examined it. It looked ordinary enough. When he rolled the head back the eyes closed, and when he moved the head forward the eyes opened again.

Now we're onto something! he said to himself.

He examined a few other boxes in the area. One of them held a consignment of wooden trains, another toy PPG pistols, a third the novelty of light-weight spheres that popped between the fingers when pressed, expelling air.

Someone was approaching.

Quickly, Sheridan put things back the way they had been, keeping one of each of the contraband toys. He retreated to his hiding spot, stowing the three toys with his trench coat and then turning to watch as a tall man approached the contraband toys. The man dug into one of the boxes and produced a train, then left.

Waiting a moment, Sheridan slipped out of his hiding spot and followed.

He kept to the shadows at first, moving from boxes to crates as the figure moved deeper into Down Below. At first there was no one around, and Sheridan was sure that if the man turned around he would be spotted. But the man did not turn around, and hesitated only once, when he seemed unsure of which direction to turn.

Soon there were people around, though, and before long they were surrounded by throngs.

The man headed for a lift, and Sheridan followed inconspicuously.

The captain waited for the man to board, then noted that it stopped at the Zocalo.

He followed, but when he arrived the man was nowhere to be seen.

On a hunch he headed left—and nearly bumped into the man, who had stopped to examine something in a stall before moving on.

Sheridan turned away, noting that the man still held the toy train.

The captain kept a discreet distance, pretending to examine a tray of dried foods when the man suddenly stopped, looking around as if expecting someone.

There was a blur of motion by the man, who then walked off.

Without the toy train, Sheridan noticed.

What—

Darting his eyes around, Sheridan looked for the source of the blur—and saw a small boy moving off, clutching the train.

In a few moments the boy had met up with two adults, dressed for travel, bags in tow. The woman took the boy by the hand and they sauntered off.

Sheridan followed them to their destination: Docking Bay 4, where they boarded a ship for Mars.

So that's how they do it! Sheridan said to himself. As he retreated from the docking area he saw two more families with children board the flight. One child clutched a doll, another a toy PPG pistol.

The security guard checking passengers laughed when the child held the PPG up and said, ''Bang!''

''Billy—don't bother the man!'' the boy's mother scolded, taking the child's toy and putting it in her bag.

Pleased with himself, Sheridan moved off, making his way back to the area in Down Below where the toys were hidden.

Feeling very much the spy, he scaled a sturdy pile of crates, settling himself on top with a view of the area, and watched as four more figures arrived to remove toys.

The key now was to discover how the other end of the operation worked. If Delenn didn't show up in a couple of hours he'd follow one of the adult figures and see where that led him. Perhaps after delivering a toy to a child the messengers went back to a central location to meet up with their boss?

Heck—this was fun!

His stomach began to rumble, and he realized he hadn't eaten since this morning. He thought about the dried foods he'd stopped to examine in the Zocalo, and wished now that he had purchased something.

Even spies had to eat, didn't they?

After enduring another twenty minutes of growing hunger, he suddenly remembered that there was a fruit bar in one of the pockets of his trench coat.

Unable to think of anything else, he made his way down the pile of crates and fished out the coat.

He was reaching into the pocket to remove the fruit bar when he felt something poke into his back and a harsh voice said, "Been spying on us, eh?"

When he turned around, something hard flashed across his face—and he met blackness.

CHAPTER 40

SUDDENLY things seemed very clear to Vir Cotto.
Marrying Lyndisty at this time would be like
death—so he might as well die beforehand!

The decision came almost as a relief to him. Since
his life was worthless anyway, he might as well
throw it away on a good cause.

He would free Londo, and save the Narn
homeworld, and be dead, and not have to marry
Lyndisty!

Perfect!

Of course, he *would* be dead, so it wasn't quite
perfect—but death was preferable to marriage, was
it not?

Yes!

Singing to himself, he examined the ruins of what
had been Lyndisty's present: a delicate crystal sun
suspended from a beautiful crystal tree. A present
would have been expected, and this was a pretty one.
Perhaps he would have it delivered to her after he
was dead so that she could remember him by what
he was at the moment: a shattered man.

A dead man.

He continued to sing, if only because everything was so clear to him now. Free Londo, then die.

That simple.

Free Londo tomorrow night: He had already made arrangements with two of the best trackers on the planet, strictly freelance and nonpolitical, who would quietly find the Narns' hideout and report back to him tomorrow night. He would then go alone, either free Londo by force or guile (probably guile) or offer himself up as a hostage in Londo's place.

Die: Once he had effected Londo's release, the Narns would surely kill him. But he would be dead.

And: Avoid Lyndisty's gala the following night.

Simple as one, two, three.

He continued to sing, because now that everything was clear to him there was nothing to worry about!

Behind him, his communications screen went on, and when he accepted the message he nearly jumped out of his skin to hear Lyndisty's voice.

"Vir!"

He turned, still holding the bag of glass pieces. The bag sagged over, and the pieces trickled out onto the floor, making a tinkling sound.

"Vir—what is that?" Lyndisty coaxed sweetly.

Vir, still in shock, looked at the pile of glass shards. "Oh, nothing, just a—"

"Present for me?" She frowned. "But it's broken!"

"I . . . yes, it is."

"I'm sure they'll replace it, if you bring it back. What was it?"

Vir was about to tell her when she halted him. "Don't tell me! Give it to me when you see me tomorrow night!"

Something she said set off alarm bells in Vir's head.

"Tomorrow night?"

"That's why I'm calling you, Vir, dear—the gala's been changed to tomorrow night!"

"But I couldn't possibly—"

She sighed. "It was father's fault, really. He had forgotten a business engagement that he just can't get out of. So the entire thing has been moved to tomorrow night!"

"But—"

She formed a pout. "You'll be here, won't you? If anything, the guest list is even *larger* now!"

"La—larger?"

"Hundreds of guests! And all for you! For . . . us!"

"Lyndisty, I ca—" He stopped, looked at her, and nodded. "I'll be there, Lyndisty."

"Good! And I can't wait to see what you've bought me!"

She signed off, leaving Vir to stare at the pile of glass shards that had been Lyndisty's present.

Just like me, Vir thought. *Broken into little pieces.*

A dead man.

CHAPTER 41

Now what was she supposed to do?

Like a good spy, Delenn had followed John Sheridan and his captor until they reached what John—Agent Y—would no doubt call the captor's "hideout." This was deep in Down Below, in a section even more remote than that in which they had been searching for the toys.

It was only serendipity that had caused her to find John again. She had been about to give up and report her find to Zack in security when something told her to try their original spot one more time. She had arrived just in time to see John being carried away by two strangers.

So she had followed, and here she was, outside "SMALL" 's headquarters, or whatever—

But now what?

Rescue John herself?

That would be foolish—and besides, the game had gone much too far already. With her discovery that weapons parts were being hidden in toys and smuggled to Mars, this game had entered the realm of seriousness.

Now that she knew where John was being held, she had to get to security as soon as possible.

That was her only course of action.

She turned away—and walked right into the largest man she had ever seen in her life.

"Can I help you?" the giant snarled.

"No, I—"

But a moment later she was lifted into the air by the man's huge hands, as if she herself were a doll, and carried toward the hideout's entrance.

CHAPTER 42

GARIBALDI couldn't believe their continuing good luck.

Not only were they allowed to see G'Kar—but they were left alone with him in G'Kar's tiny, bleak cell while the emperor and his cronies cooed over their new gem purchases. And, with the amount of alcohol that had been consumed by the emperor and everyone around him while they were making their sales, it was quite possible that they could walk G'Kar out right under Cartagia's nose and he wouldn't even know it.

The one problem seemed to be that G'Kar had been drugged.

Getting the cell door open had been easy enough—one thing Garibaldi had learned was that there really wasn't such a thing as security. Just about any lock could be opened—with the right tool, which Michael now pocketed as he quietly opened the cell door and went in.

Franklin followed, after Ivanova, acting as lookout in the hallway, gave her the signal that everything was still clear.

"What's wrong with him?" Garibaldi whispered, regarding the Narn, who lay prone on the floor, seemingly asleep.

"He's been drugged, looks like," Franklin determined, after failing to wake G'Kar. "Maybe something they gave him for the pain—though I doubt it." He winced. "Look at the welts on his back. I bet they gave him something to make him feel even worse."

Garibaldi shook his head, as G'Kar turned slightly, moaned, and muttered something in his stupor.

Franklin got a hand around the Narn's shoulder and tried to get him to stand up.

"Come on, G'Kar—give me a little help, okay?"

G'Kar opened his sleepy eyes and stared into Garibaldi's face.

"A dream . . ." he said. "A bad dream . . ."

"You said it," Franklin agreed, as Garibaldi supported the Narn from the opposite side and they began to walk him out of the cell.

In the hallway, Ivanova whispered, "Quick! They've moved into another room—a vault or something. We can get him out now!"

"That's the plan," Garibaldi said, and now they quickly walked and dragged G'Kar down the hallway, across the audience chamber, and out the opposite doorway toward the front of the palace.

There was a single guard ahead. Ivanova rushed toward him, and before the guard turned to see G'Kar, Susan said something to him and he ran away from them.

"What did you tell him?" Garibaldi asked.

Ivanova, returning to help with G'Kar, said, "I told him the emperor was drunk and giving out emeralds in the back of the palace."

"For all we know," Garibaldi commented, "he might be doing that!"

They bore G'Kar, who seemed to rouse himself a little as night air hit him, down the steps of the palace and away.

In no time at all, they had the Narn in Garibaldi's quarters, asleep on his bed.

Ivanova looked down at his fitful rest. "Poor G'Kar."

"Well, he's away from that madman now," Garibaldi said. "And it's a good thing we planned on these backup quarters beforehand. As soon as Cartagia finds that we've sprung G'Kar, there'll be imperial guards swarming around our old place like ants on a mound of sugar."

Ivanova nodded. "Time to call Captain Sheridan and get out of here, don't you think?"

"It can't be too soon for me," Garibaldi answered.

But when Garibaldi contacted Babylon 5, he got a worried Zack on the line.

"What's wrong?" Garibaldi asked.

"Just about everything," Zack answered. "The captain went off with Ambassador Delenn. They were supposed to check in every half day, but he missed the last two check-ins. He modified his link, and I'm afraid he may not be able to get in touch now."

"What's he up to?" Garibaldi asked.

Zack told him, and Garibaldi smiled. "Couldn't resist a little action himself, eh?"

"Right," Zack said, "but he could have picked a better time. When Captain Sheridan left things were quiet, but now they're heating up again. It looked like everything was fine in the Euphrates sector, but now we're getting reports that there may be big trouble there after all. And the rioting has started up again."

"In short, you need the captain and he can't be found, right?"

"Right. And there's bad news for you, too. The ship Commander Ivanova wanted to pick you up near your jump gate in hyperspace had to leave its spot when a Centauri battle cruiser got a little too close."

"Which means you can't get us out of here tonight."

"We can get the ship back into position tomorrow."

"All right," Garibaldi said, "here's what you do. Take as many people as you can spare from riot control, and get them out looking for the captain. Have him call me as soon as he's found. In the meantime, get that ship back into position as fast as you can, ready to pick us up on Centauri Prime at a moment's notice. Got that?"

"Got it," Zack replied. "I take it you've got G'Kar?"

Garibaldi looked at the prone Narn. "We've got him, and we're ready to get him out of here."

After signing off, he said to himself, "If we can figure out a way."

CHAPTER 43

"AND who is *this* one?" the bald man questioned, in surprise.

The giant lowered Delenn to the floor. Trying to regain her dignity, she smoothed her garments and said, "I am Delenn. I am Minbari ambassador to Babylon 5, and I demand that I be freed at once." She indicated Captain Sheridan, who was tied to a chair, seemingly unconscious. "And he is John Sheridan, captain of Babylon 5. I demand that he be freed, also."

"Sure," the bald man snickered, in a mocking tone. "And I'm Captain Kidd, and the tall guy there is Shazam." He laughed. "Now, why don't you tell me who the two of you really are?"

"I've told you who we are," Delenn insisted. "And I know who you are."

"Really?" the bald man retorted incredulously. "And who would that be?"

"You are smugglers. Captain Sheridan capriciously considers you members of SMALL."

The bald man snorted. "What the hell is SMALL?"

"A spy organization. A mere fancy." Delenn racked her memory. "It stands for Secret Martian Allies. Of course, John said that this was just a game, but it is obvious that Captain Sheridan and I are not playing a game anymore."

The third man in the room, a short fellow who sat in another chair and spent most of his time looking at his nails, looked up now and blurted out a laugh. Delenn saw that he was missing many teeth.

"The dame's koo-koo!" the short man spat.

The bald man agreed, "Sure sounds like it." To Delenn he said, "Actually, my name's Mitchell, and you're starting to piss me off."

The giant took a step toward Delenn, but Mitchell held up his hand.

"Not yet. You can break both of them in half later. First I want to find out what they know—and why she's dressed in the funny getup."

"This was part of the game, my spy trench coat," Delenn explained. She reached into her pocket, produced her dark glasses. "These were part of the game, also. Perhaps you will believe me now when I tell you who we are. And I demand that you free us immediately."

"She *is* koo-koo!" the short man reiterated, pausing again from his examination of his nails.

"Could be," Mitchell said.

"Hey, can you imagine if they really *were* who she says they are? That'd put us in some really deep doo-doo, wouldn't it?"

Now both Mitchell and the short man guffawed. The giant grinned lopsidedly.

"Lady," Mitchell declared when the laughter had

subsided, "about the last thing I'm going to do is let you go. And I'll tell you what's going to happen next. In a few hours you'll be on your way to Mars in a cargo hold, in a crate without any air in it. But that'll be okay, because you won't need any air anyway, because you'll be dead."

Mitchell and the short man laughed again, and this time the giant joined in, with a chuckle of his own.

CHAPTER 44

"I HAVE wonderful news—though not necessarily for you, Mollari," L'Kan announced.

Londo Mollari, tired, hungry, nearly frantic from the soreness that continued to plague his buttocks, snapped, "I don't care about your news!"

L'Kan smiled. "That's too bad, because it concerns you, too."

"What is it, then?" Londo pressed, just to make the Narn spit out his news and then shut up.

"It seems G'Kar has broken out of captivity."

Instantly, the pain in Mollari's buttocks receded, as the much larger, sudden pain in his mind took over.

"What! That's impossible! You said so yourself!"

"Yes, I thought it would be impossible to free G'Kar by force from the imperial palace—but apparently it has been done."

"Who did this?" Londo demanded. "Your men? If so, you must return him at once—"

"In fact," L'Kan interrupted, "he was freed by three of your own people."

"Centauris! That is insanity!"

"The news is all over the empire. It seems Cartagia let them walk out right from under his nose. The news channels are not allowed to say that, of course. According to them, there was a great battle, during which Cartagia himself was wounded in the defense of the empire, and Narns, disguised as Centauri, battled their way through hordes of imperial guards sworn to protect the emperor and all of Centauri Prime. As you yourself realize, as would anyone with half a brain, it would be nearly impossible for a Narn to impersonate a Centauri—therefore, we must conclude that three of your own people kidnapped G'Kar."

"For what purpose?"

"That is something we aren't sure of. Perhaps for ransom, perhaps for other reasons. If it is for ransom, I have already been authorized to give them what they want so that we may deliver G'Kar back to the Narn homeworld. If they plan to harm him in any way, we will track them down and take G'Kar by force, if necessary."

"This is not possible!" Londo shouted. "I've told you, G'Kar must stay where he is! *He* would tell you that, if he were here!"

L'Kan smiled. "Soon he *will* be here, Mollari. And then I will offer him the singular pleasure of slitting your throat himself."

CHAPTER 45

THE dawn of a new day.

Perhaps, Vir Cotto thought, *my last.*

Sighing heavily, he pulled himself out of bed. His hair was mussed; he scarcely cared and made no effort to preen. He wore his bedclothes—perhaps he would wear them all day, and wear them to Lyndisty's gala tonight.

Perhaps he would wear them when he threw himself off the nearest high wall.

Sighing again, he answered his communications screen by not bothering to look at who had called him.

"We've made progress on your needs, Vir Cotto," a vaguely recognizable voice reported.

Barely interested, Vir let his gaze wander up to the screen.

"Oh!" Vir cried, suddenly interested.

It was one of the two trackers he had hired to find where Londo Mollari was being held.

"You've found him?" Vir asked.

"We know the vicinity where he is being held," the man answered. He was furtive, and his hair crest was short, making him, of course, not a higher grade of Centauri—but he had the highest qualifications for what he did, and was known as completely discreet.

"That sounds . . . vague," Vir responded.

"It is," the man said. Vir saw a slight smile.

"Is it a matter of money?" Vir asked.

"It's always a matter of money," the other asserted. "But there's something else."

Vir waited, then asked, "You *will* be able to get me close to him, won't you?"

"Possibly . . ."

"Possibly?" Vir repeated, trying not to let new panic creep into his voice. "Our arrangement was that you find him, and then you get me close."

"I know that. And I always keep my word. It's just that . . ." For a moment the man's slight smile turned to something else—something almost like embarrassment.

"What happened?" Vir asked. "And where's your partner Chilo?"

"Chilo is dead."

"Dead?" Vir's voice rose a half octave.

"He was . . . killed during the operation. Not your fault, at all. And nothing has been compromised. It's only that . . ."

Again Vir waited, and this time before he could say anything the man blurted out what was on his mind.

"I was . . . wondering if you would pick up the tab for Chilo's . . . *arrangements.*"

"His funeral?"

"Yes. I . . ."

Suddenly everything was clear to Vir. Immediately he became his best diplomatic self, and said, "Of course. Consider it done, as a . . . bonus."

"Thank you." Immediately the other had become businesslike again.

"And when will—" Vir began.

"I'll be in touch with you," the man said. "It won't be long before I can get you close."

"But how will you know where I am?"

Again the slight smile returned.

"I'll know where you are. It's what I do. Just be ready."

The screen went blank before Vir could say another word.

Vir stared at the blank screen with his mouth open for a few moments.

Amazing. What he had just seen was amazing.

For now, the depth of his problems lessened with the prospect of action. Even though there was a good chance he would die trying to rescue Londo, at least he was *doing* something now.

But still, what he had just seen . . .

Vir shook his head at the way Centauri treated one another. The man on the screen just now had been embarassed to ask for a bonus to bury his dead partner—not because he felt bad about Chilo's death, but because he felt bad about the prospect of having to pay for the man's funeral himself.

Vir shook his head again.

Just amazing.

CHAPTER 46

THERE was a fading dream of the homeworld, blasted red sky that melted into gray as G'Kar heard very familiar voices, and then woke up.

He opened his eyes.

Could it be?

Could he be home?

But no, he was not—he was in Centauri living quarters of some sort—the same type of decadent furnishings he had become all too used to during his hellish stay on this hellish planet.

But those voices . . .

"Gari . . . baldi?" G'Kar said tentatively, sitting up and rubbing his head.

Someone walked into the room, but it was not Garibaldi. It was a rather ugly Centauri—but weren't they all ugly?

The Centauri spoke—in Garibaldi's voice.

"So, G'Kar—how's the headache? Feeling better?"

G'Kar's mouth dropped open, and now that he looked more closely . . .

"Is it *you*, Garibaldi?"

"In the flesh." The disguised Babylon 5 security chief looked down at himself. "Or something like that."

Behind Garibaldi appeared two other figures. G'Kar studied them intently.

"Care to guess?" The voice of Susan Ivanova resounded from the mouth of a bald-headed Centauri female.

"Ivanova." G'Kar studied the other figure, and after a few moments concluded, "And . . . Dr. Franklin?"

"Right!" Franklin nodded.

"As far as you're concerned," Garibaldi said, "as long as we're still on Centauri Prime, which won't be long I hope, you have to refer to us as Pir Chetski, Mita Cornova, and Jato Mindara."

As if really waking from his dream now, G'Kar's face showed real shock.

"No! How did I get here! You must bring me back!"

Quickly, Garibaldi filled G'Kar in on what had happened, ending with, "It'll take the imperial guards a bit of time to track us down, but by then we'll be on our way back to Babylon 5."

"But you don't understand!" G'Kar protested. "I can't return to Babylon 5! I must stay here!"

"And be tortured, and probably killed, by Emperor Cartagia?" Garibaldi shook his head.

"I can't explain it to you! But you must believe me! In fact, the fate of the Narn homeworld relies on it!"

Garibaldi looked at his two "Centauri" companions, then back at G'Kar.

"You're not saying this because you're drugged or anything, are you?"

"No," G'Kar denied emphatically.

Ivanova asked, "Or because one of your relatives is being held hostage on Narn, something like that?"

"I tell you again, no. As you know, all of Narn is being held hostage. And if you do not return me to Cartagia, that bondage may last forever."

Franklin was studying G'Kar intently. "Let me run some tests," he suggested. "Just to make sure he hasn't been . . . altered in any way."

"Run any tests you like," G'Kar consented, "but I assure you that I am perfectly sane, and very much myself."

Ivanova looked at Franklin. "Make it quick," she said. "Because if we really do have to return him to Cartagia, we've got a lot of fast dancing to do."

Franklin nodded, and turned to G'Kar.

"Ready?" he asked.

An hour later, Franklin pronounced G'Kar wholly himself.

"He may be insane," he reported, "but if he is I can't detect it. He's been abused physically, and he's been given some drugs, but nothing that's been done to him has altered the fact that he's G'Kar."

The Narn regarded them quietly from where he sat on his bed.

Ivanova sighed. "You sure about this, G'Kar?"

"Surer than I've ever been of anything in my life."

"And you won't tell us what's going on?"

"Only that things must be this way. Do you really think I *want* to return to that madman Cartagia? It is only that it must be."

Ivanova consulted with her two companions, then said, "All right, we'll take you back. But God help us if we're doing the wrong thing."

"You're doing the right thing," G'Kar assured her. Welling up with pride and emotion, he continued, "And I will never forget what you have done. You have risked your lives for me, which is the greatest gift one can give another."

"You gave me that gift yourself—which is what got you into this mess in the first place," Garibaldi added.

"You are true friends. But if you return me to Cartagia, you will be even truer friends, not only of me but of all Narn."

"All right," Garibaldi agreed quietly. "But we won't sleep well at night, knowing you're being tortured—"

"It will not last forever," G'Kar said. "And better things will come of it."

"I hope so," Garibaldi said. "And now before we get you back on the streets, I've got to make a call home, and get us out of here. Hopefully there's a ship waiting in hyperspace, but it looks like it will just be taking the three of us home."

G'Kar held up a hand.

"Mr. Garibaldi, could I ask another great favor of you?"

Garibaldi said, "Just ask."

"Could you hold off on that communication for a

little while? There is something else that must be done, and I think you may be the ones to do it."

"What's that, G'Kar?"

"Vir Cotto informed me that Londo Mollari was abducted by the Narn commandos who were sent to free me. I want you to free Londo Mollari from the commandos, and make them go back to Narn."

Garibaldi turned to Franklin and asked, "Are you sure he's not nuts?"

"He's not," Franklin conceded, "but he sure sounds like it."

Ivanova spoke up. "You want us to help Londo? Is that what you're saying?"

"That's right, Commander Ivanova, that's what I'm saying."

Ivanova shook her head. "This is getting nuttier by the second."

CHAPTER 47

ZACK had always hoped for advancement in his career—but the last thing he thought he would be doing when he woke up this morning, and the last thing he *wanted* to be doing, was trying to keep Babylon 5 under control.

Things were going smoothly here in the Observation Dome. Command and Control had the station's basic operations in hand. But as far as security went, his responsibility, that was another matter. The riots had not subsided; in fact they had gotten worse, causing Zack to pull needed people off the detail searching for Captain Sheridan and Ambassador Delenn and throw them into antiriot details.

The most bothersome thing was that he hadn't heard from either the captain or the ambassador in more than a day—and that was a day too long. They could be anywhere by now, and in any kind of trouble, and, well, Zack felt helpless.

Now he knew what it was like to run things—and, boy, now he understood why the captain, the commander, and Security Chief Garibaldi often looked the way they did: haggard, tired, and just plain over-whelmed.

"Zack?"

"Yes, Rochford, what is it?" he inquired into his link, answering the security officer heading up the search for Sheridan and Delenn.

"We may have gotten a break," Rochford reported.

"What did you find?"

"It's not what we found, particularly, but what we heard. More than one person swears they saw the captain in the Zocalo area yesterday. The thing that makes me believe the reports is that they all said he was dressed funny—in black pants and a black turtleneck."

"That was definitely him," Zack said. "Anything else?"

"I'm afraid that's it. One of the witnesses says the captain was following a little boy and his parents."

"A little boy? Did the kid have a toy or something?"

"I don't know, Zack."

"Go back and interview that witness again. The captain was investigating something having to do with toys."

Rochford said, "Right. This person might end up being a big help. She said that after she recognized the captain she followed him for a while out of curiosity, and saw that the family with the little boy boarded a ship."

"Check the whole story out and get back to me."

"Will do."

Zack signed off and sat in the nearest chair.

But he couldn't relax.

Man, running things was *hard*.

CHAPTER 48

Ra'Nik reported to L'Kan, "The body was removed, but I'm sure that the Centauri was dead."

"Good," L'Kan said. "I'm not surprised that we have been discovered. We will simply move more deeply into the tunnels, and watch for any further actions against our present location. It may be that we do not have much time left."

Ra'Nik nodded. "It may be that we will have to execute Mollari soon."

L'Kan said, "It greatly disturbs me that this Vir Cotto has done nothing to make the exchange. I thought he would have immediately tried to deal with those who had freed G'Kar. Perhaps a dead Mollari will help convince him that we mean to do everything necessary to get what we want." He paused. "It also greatly disturbs me that we have heard nothing about those who have taken G'Kar."

"This troubles me, too," Ra'Nik agreed. "Their motivations remain unclear."

"We will deal with them, and do what has to be done," L'Kan concluded. "As I said, time is short."

Ra'Nik looked at the sleeping form of Londo Mollari, who sat slumped in his chair. The ambassador moaned in his sleep and sought unconsciously to shift the weight from his buttocks.

"And time," Ra'Nik said, without a trace of compassion, "is especially short for *him*."

CHAPTER 49

"As I've tried to explain to you," Captain Sheridan said, "half the station will be looking for us by now."

The bald man, Mitchell, laughed. "Half the station is too busy with the rioting." He grinned. "And I hear there's more trouble in the Euphrates sector."

"What!" Sheridan's face reddened. "Then you've *got* to let me go!"

"So you can save the universe?" The short man stopped examining his nails and smirked.

"Look," Mitchell said, his smile fading. "I don't believe you're who you say you are, and that's that. I think you're trying to horn in and either blackmail me or extort me. And since I don't like either of those possibilities, I'm going to get rid of you. Permanently."

Sheridan indicated Delenn. "At least let her go."

Now Mitchell grinned. "How can I? She's with you, and she claims I'm the head of an organization called SMALL. The only thing worse than an extortionist is a kook!"

Laughing, Mitchell, the short man, and the giant left the room, sealing the door behind them.

"Well, Agent Y," Delenn asked when they were alone, "do you have any ideas?"

"No, Agent X, I don't," Sheridan responded, miserably. "The best we can hope for is that Zack's people find us. And," he added, "I do think it's time to drop our little game."

Delenn gave him her slight, ironic smile. "But I was just beginning to enjoy it!"

The captain's face filled with wonder. "You actually acted like that fellow Mitchell really was the head of SMALL?"

"Yes! I thought it might confuse him."

Sheridan shook his head. "All it seemed to do was make him mad."

Delenn's face lost its playfulness and became serious. "For that I am sorry, John."

"It's all right, Delenn."

"Does your head hurt much?" she asked.

"Only when I laugh."

"Then you must not laugh." She became quizzical. "And what, exactly, is a 'kook'?"

"Actually," Sheridan mused, "the word 'kook' sometimes describes you to perfection."

CHAPTER 50

B<small>Y</small> covering G'Kar with a cloak and treating him like a slave, it was easy to move through the streets undetected.

As they neared the imperial palace, though, only Garibaldi accompanied the Narn. Ivanova and Franklin prepared to stay back.

"Be careful, Pir," Ivanova warned.

"I have no intention of doing otherwise." Garibaldi nodded, raising his voice in admonition of G'Kar when a Centauri citizen wandered close. When the woman had moved on, Garibaldi said, "You're absolutely sure about this, G'Kar?"

"I have never been so sure of anything in my life," the Narn admitted.

Garibaldi shrugged. "All right, then. Here goes nothing."

"We'll keep a lookout," Ivanova said.

Garibaldi and G'Kar moved slowly toward the steps of the imperial palace.

"Those guys do the job?" Garibaldi asked, nodding toward the group of imperial guards at the top of the steps.

"They'll do nicely, yes. It was good of you to accompany me this far. I fear that if I had wandered the streets alone until captured, I may have been beaten to death before I was returned to the palace."

"Where you'll be beaten by a mad emperor instead," Garibaldi muttered bitterly.

"Yes . . ." G'Kar said. "When we get to the bottom of the steps, I suggest that you leave me. I will go up alone."

"You know I feel rotten about this, G'Kar."

"I know that. And it heartens me."

They reached the steps, and Garibaldi blew out a breath.

"Well, here we are."

G'Kar took his hand in a firm grip. "I will never forget what you have done."

"So you say. But I still feel rotten."

The Narn unclasped his hand and turned without another word to slowly make his way up the steps.

By the time Garibaldi had reached his companions, G'Kar had nearly made it to the top of the steps.

"So far they haven't seen him," Ivanova reported.

Garibaldi joined their surveillance. "Looks like that's about to end."

As these words left Garibaldi's mouth, G'Kar let his cloak drop and stood meters away from the conversing imperial guards. He stood proudly, and must have said something, because the guards abruptly turned and regarded him.

Then there was a shout and the guards surrounded him.

"I don't think I can watch this," Garibaldi said. Yet he could not look away.

G'Kar stood tall for a moment, but then was driven to the steps by blows from the imperial guards. More guards rushed out from within the palace, and among them they began to drag the humbled Narn into the building, kicking and pummeling him as they did so.

"Let's get out of here," Ivanova said grimly. "I can't take any more of this."

Franklin had already turned away.

"Let's go," Garibaldi said, turning his back last on the sad spectacle.

Before long, they had made their way to the outskirts of the city and beheld the mining tunnel entrance that would lead them underground.

"You sure this is the place?" Garibaldi sounded skeptical.

"At first G'Kar didn't have any idea where they'd be," Ivanova answered, "but when I accessed the city maps of the tunnels, he remembered seeing similar information that had been gathered by Narn spies, just so they'd have a place of operations if they ever needed it on Centauri Prime. He remembered that they had judged this area the most secure, and isolated, of all the places they scouted. The Narn commandos will most probably be in here somewhere."

''And what exactly do we say to these fellows when we find them?'' Garibaldi inquired.

Franklin, with some sarcasm, retorted, ''We ask them, 'Please, fellas, let Londo Mollari go because G'Kar told us to tell you so.' ''

''Actually,'' Ivanova said, as they made their way toward the looming dark hole, ''I have no idea what to say.''

CHAPTER 51

L'KAN shouted in a rage, *"He has been delivered back to Cartagia!"*

Ra'Nik said, "I wish it were not so, but that is what has happened. Our sources tell us that three Centauri—presumably the same three who kidnapped him from the palace—returned G'Kar to the palace steps this morning."

Seeking to control his rage but failing, L'Kan brought his fist down on the nearest object, a table, and shattered its top. "Apparently the cowards were paid. Which leaves us back where we began."

Needing action, he strode into the next room, where Londo Mollari sat tied to his chair. After much begging he had finally been given a pillow of sorts to temper the pain in his buttocks.

Now L'Kan marched angrily up to the Centauri and yanked the pillow from beneath him.

Mollari winced, and cried, "Why have you done this?"

"I will do worse, soon!" L'Kan vowed. "If I do not hear from your toady, Vir Cotto, by this eve-

ning, your dead body will be found on the streets of
the city tomorrow.''

"Perhaps we can talk—"

"No more talk!" L'Kan shouted. "I have spo-
ken, and it will be so." He raised his fists to heaven.
"If G'Kar is not exchanged for you this night—you
will die!''

CHAPTER 52

G'KAR found it very hard to block out this kind of pain with dreams of the Narn homeworld—or any other dreams, for that matter.

For a while, he thought of Babylon 5. Before the war with the Centauri, the station had been a rather pleasant place to be. There had been tension, of course, and he had never gotten along with Londo Mollari—but the work had been interesting and, at times, fruitful. The friendships he had forged, especially with members of the human race, had both surprised and, to this day, sustained him. The humans were really a remarkable people; as fractious as any other species—and, when riled, as deadly— yet possessing a depth of loyalty and compassion that rivaled that of any other breed on any other world. Before his assignment on Babylon 5, G'Kar never would have thought he could become so close to members of another race—and here he was, in the middle of a pain he had brought on himself, only because he had, of necessity, refused the help of *humans*.

It was amazing.

And so was this agony. All other thoughts vanished into a white haze of pain, as the heat being applied to his bare soles rose up like tendrils of fire into his legs and up to his brain. He gritted his teeth and sought not to cry out, but the effort was a failure; the anguish was just too great.

"I . . . am . . . G'Kar!" he hissed out between his teeth, wanting to give Cartagia no pleasure from his agony.

"Yes, you are!" the emperor trilled. "But not for long! Soon you will be . . . *cooked* Narn!"

A ripple of laughter from the emperor's invited guests broke out and politely died. G'Kar could just see some of their faces in a ring around him.

More intense heat. He cried out, "*And you . . . are Centauri . . . dogs!*"

"Don't the Earth humans have something called a . . . hot dog?" the emperor quipped.

More laughter; more hot pain.

Suddenly Cartagia's voice grew cold, and his face loomed over G'Kar's. "I've decided I really don't care who the three Centauri are who spirited you away. I'd come to the conclusion that they were fools who thought they would get a ransom greater than their wonderful gemstones, and then got scared. They were very smart to bring you back to me, because I would have flayed them alive otherwise. So we'll forget about them—unless, of course, they're caught. What I'm most interested in is *you,* G'Kar."

Hot pain filled G'Kar's eyes. "I will . . . tell you . . . *nothing!*"

"Oh, I have no doubt of that," the emperor said,

regaining both his seat and his mild manner. To G'Kar's torturer he idly said, "Can the flame get any hotter on that thing?"

Instantly, an even hotter pain seared through G'Kar's mind and body. He could smell himself cooking.

He fought to think of other things: of home, of Babylon 5, of anything at all.

The pain tore into him again; he failed and thought only of pain.

"As I said," the emperor remarked languidly, "what I'm interested in is you, G'Kar. Not for what you know, but for what you are."

There was a pause in the emperor's speech, during which, thankfully, there came a pause in the hot agony.

Once again, Emperor Cartagia's face loomed over G'Kar. Through hot tears, the Narn saw the cold set in the madman's features, and the madness itself in his eyes.

"And what *are* you, G'Kar?" the emperor asked, rhetorically. There was dead silence in the room.

"I . . . am . . . G'Kar . . ." the Narn breathed out, in a bare whisper.

The emperor slowly shook his head.

"You are . . . *nothing*. And," he continued, his voice lightening, "you are my plaything!"

Once again pain, and no other memory, came to G'Kar.

CHAPTER 53

IN a kind of trance born of equal parts resignation and desperation, Vir Cotto mulled over what to wear. The remaining tracker he had hired, Chilo's partner, had not gotten back in touch with him. He could not execute his plan, since he didn't know where Londo was being held. He had no choice but to attend the gala.

Almost thankfully, his communications screen came on and Lyndisty's voice floated out to him.

"Vir—aren't you dressed yet?"

"I'm getting dressed now, Lyndisty." He stepped back from his wardrobe so that she could see. "Any suggestions?"

"Wear . . . that one! The one on the end!" she proposed gaily.

"Fine!" Vir snapped.

"Vir! Why do you sound so . . . strange?"

Because, he almost said, *I'm about to die and I don't care anymore.*

What he really said was, "Strange? Why, I must just be nervous!"

"Don't be! Everything will be wonderful!"

He waved at her and smiled woodenly as she signed off.

"See you soon, Vir dear!"

"Soon . . ." Vir answered, still waving his fingers as the screen went blank, before letting his smile collapse and picking not the outfit Lyndisty had indicated, which was his finest, but rather his worst outfit, which he used for menial tasks around his quarters, and which he never, until now, would ever think of wearing in public.

And soon he was making his way to this grandest of all galas. He walked, hoping that something from the sky would fall on his head and kill him, or, perhaps, a crazy person would rush out of the evening shadows and bludgeon him to death. Perhaps crazed animals roamed the night and would do him in, or a rogue PPG blast fired from blocks away would find him as its target, or . . .

But nothing untoward happened to him. The evening was fine, with a warmness perfect for a party, and a sprinkling of stars overhead like a heavenly blessing.

Up ahead he could see the glow from Lyndisty's home. The soft aura seemed to merge with the evening's stars like a soft crown under the cosmos. Already he could hear the tinkle of glasses and the sound of laughter. A hint of soft music from the band outside the house in the sculpted gardens found its way to him on the subtle breeze.

If this had been anyone else's party he would have looked forward to it.

"Vir!"

She was waiting for him on the steps and came running lightly down to meet him. In the soft glow from the gala she was beautiful, with her eyes achingly large and limpid. A circlet of tiny flowers rested upon her bare head like a princess's crown. For a moment he was enchanted.

"Lyndisty—"

She frowned, seeing him in the light.

"You didn't wear the outfit I picked for you! Why, Vir, this outfit looks *awful*!"

"Yes, it does," he admitted without energy.

"We must see what we can do to fix you up!" Lyndisty said. "After all, this is your big night!"

"Big night," Vir parroted, again without enthusiasm.

She turned and ran into the house, leaving a glow of inner light behind.

"Hey, Cotto!" a voice called out of the darkness.

Idly, Vir looked into the shadows. Chilo's partner was there, and emerged slowly and cautiously.

"It's time," the man said.

"Now?"

"Now or never. At considerable risk to life and limb, I went back and discovered where they've moved their hiding place to. They're going to execute Mollari tonight. It's now or never."

"Can I choose never?"

"Your choice, my friend. You're the one with the credits."

Resignedly, Vir conceded, "You'll take me there?"

The other laughed. "Are you kidding? If I go

back there again they'll spill my guts. You're on your own.''

''But how—?''

The man stepped out of the shadows, pressing something into Vir's hand.

''It's a map,'' he explained. ''It'll get you there.''

''I suppose I should say thank you—''

''Just make sure the credits are in my account.''

''It's been taken care of. And the bonus. You see, I don't expect to return from—''

But the man was gone, into the shadows and beyond them, and Vir turned to see that Lyndisty was back, with a beautiful outfit, no doubt borrowed from her father, draped over one arm. Behind her, her parents beamed, mother and father, proud, exquisitely attired, waiting for Vir to dress and enter. Behind *them,* a throng of people were massed, looking out at Vir expectantly. They looked carnivorous. Somewhere deep in the residence, amid the expensive artwork and a thousand other objects purchased on the backs and blood of thousands of dead Narns, a *second* orchestra, distinct from the one in the gardens, began to play a trumpet voluntary. The night was hushed, expectant . . .

Vir knew what would happen next: after he dressed in Lyndisty's father's clothes, he would be ushered into the house and feted, and fed, and then fed to Lyndisty's parents on a bed of matrimony. Somewhere between the eighth and ninth courses of an eleven-course meal, Lyndisty's father would rise with mock solemnity, raise his glass, and make the announcement of the impending marriage. Vir had no doubt that the date, unbeknownst to him, had already been set—hadn't everything else?

And he would sit there, and smile, and be, for all intents and purposes, dead.

"I'm sorry, Lyndisty, but there's something I really must do!" Vir blurted, thrusting the bag he had brought into her hand and turning away even as she, face beaming with the look of love, held out her father's cloak to him.

Vir was a few steps away from her when he stopped, turned around, and walked back. He pulled her out of the doorway, and out of earshot of her parents and the guests.

"Vir—" she began.

"Please, just listen to me," Vir insisted. "It would be cruel of me to just walk away from you now, but since I'm probably going to die tonight anyway—"

Again he held up his hand for her silence, as her eyes went wide with concern.

"Just listen! Please!" Vir pleaded. "Since I'm probably going to die tonight, I want you to know that it would have been very difficult for me to marry you anyway."

"But, Vir, we can overcome anything—"

"There's something I don't know if I could ever overcome, Lyndisty. And it's the way your parents found their fame and honor. What they did to those people on Narn—I don't know if I could ever get past that. There. I've said it. Now I have to go."

He heard her cry out once and then again, a lonely bird's call on a beautiful evening, as he hurried away, dead one way as well as another, into the night to save Londo.

In the night, as hushed, shocked voices began to whisper and then chatter behind her, Lyndisty stood in mournful shock.

"Vir!" she called out again, hearing her cry echo and die in the stillness of what was to have been the most perfect evening of her life.

She felt her mother's gentle hands fall on her shoulders, but did not turn around. Hot tears were streaming down her cheeks.

"He—"

"I know, dear," her mother comforted her. "I told you they're *all* beasts."

Her mother's gentle hands, words, retreated.

The chattering voices retreated, deeper into the house, to eat, to dance, to drink at what would become, in effect, a funeral party.

A funeral for Lyndisty's dreams.

She sadly opened and turned over the bag Vir had given her—and watched a stream of broken glass pieces fall, reflecting fairy nightlight, to be broken into even smaller shards as they struck the ground with tinkling sounds, something like gay laughter.

CHAPTER 54

SHERIDAN had thought about one day revisiting Mars—but not like this.

"Delenn, can you breathe?"

"Yes, John, I can breathe. But the question becomes: for how long?"

"Precisely," Sheridan said. "If this container really *is* airtight, like Mitchell claimed, then whatever air is in here won't last very long."

"Do you think we are still on Babylon 5?"

"That's hard to—"

As if in answer, the container shifted violently, turning them from a horizontal to a vertical position and tumbling the boxes within the container around them. Bound hand and foot, Delenn and Sheridan suddenly found themselves side by side in the darkness.

"Hell of a way to travel," he quipped.

There was more movement, and Sheridan estimated that they were once more being moved.

"I get the feeling we're being loaded onto a Mars-bound freighter just about now," Sheridan observed.

"Shall we try to yell and pound again?"

"Why not?" Sheridan replied. "We haven't found a way out. Yelling was ineffective before—but maybe it'll help now."

They pushed their way between boxes along the floor of the container to the wall.

"Help!" Delenn shouted.

Sheridan, for his own part, pounded with his bound fists on the confining wall of the container.

Outside, they heard a faint sound.

It was a voice—Mitchell's.

"Comfy in there?" Mitchell taunted, and there was muted laughter from what sounded like the short man. "You can yell all you want, since we're going with you to Mars. As soon as I get you in the hold, Murphy and I are going up front and having ourselves a beer. I estimate you'll be dead in less than an hour. So, like I said, holler all you want!"

There was more laughter, diminishing.

The crate was jarred again and again, then tilted over onto its side once more, throwing Delenn on top of the captain.

"I'm sorry to be put in such a position, captain," Delenn apologized.

Sheridan laughed grimly as they adjusted themselves side by side once more.

"It's quite all right, Delenn. But I think it's time we came up with a better plan than yelling and banging on the container."

"That would be a good idea," Delenn concurred.

There was silence in the confined space, and then Sheridan said in the darkness, "Do you have a good plan yet?"

"No," Delenn answered. "Do you?"

"No."

Again, silence.

"I think . . ." Delenn finally began.

"Yes?"

"I think," Delenn said, with finality, "that it's time we become secret agents again, and get ourselves out of this predicament."

"I totally agree, Agent X. Do you have any ideas?"

"Unfortunately, Agent Y, I do not," she said.

"What would James Bond do, I wonder?" Sheridan mused.

"Yes, that is a good way of thinking. What would this James Blonde do?"

"That's Bond, not Blonde," Sheridan corrected her.

"Sorry."

Once again there was silence.

There was a jolt, and Sheridan knew that they were now free of Babylon 5. In a little while there was a rush of movement, which told them that they had entered the Epsilon jump gate and were on their way to Mars.

"I think," Delenn said solemnly, as the air in the enclosed, sealed, airtight container began to sour and they suddenly found their breathing shallower, harder, "that I know what James Bond, in such a situation as this, would do."

"What's that?" Sheridan asked.

"I'm afraid," Delenn concluded, "that he would perish."

CHAPTER 55

It wasn't long before Ivanova, Garibaldi, and Franklin were hopelessly lost.

"How do they build these tunnels—like groundhogs?" Garibaldi quipped. "There doesn't seem to be any rhyme or reason."

"Since we're in a mining area, I would guess they just head for where the minerals are," Ivanova answered.

"Couldn't these Narns hide in something with less twists and turns, like an old Earth subway tunnel?"

"At least they keep everything well lit," Franklin chimed in, with mock cheerfulness.

Up ahead was yet another split in the passageway. When they reached it, they were, for what seemed the fiftieth time, faced with making a decision.

"I say right," Ivanova advised.

"And I say we stay left," Garibaldi said.

"So far, left has gotten us nowhere," Ivanova countered.

"And you'd rather be in a different brand of no-where?" Garibaldi answered. "Neither has right."

Franklin, trying to moderate, asked, "Why don't we just alternate?"

They both turned on him.

"No way," Ivanova responded.

"My way or none," Garibaldi added.

The emergency signal on Garibaldi's link, which he had hidden on his thigh, went off, sending a tremble through his skin that could not be heard but could be felt.

"The link just went off," he said. "Excuse me a second."

He fished into his Centauri garments to remove the communications device.

"Pir Chetski here," Garibaldi spoke into the link.

Zack's voice came back, puzzled. "Who?"

"Sorry. Garibaldi here."

Zack recovered, and continued, "Chief, we've got big problems here. I'm afraid we're going to have to initiate your emergency return plan, whether you're ready or not."

"What's wrong?"

"The station's going to hell is what's wrong!" Zack confessed. They could hear the strain in his voice. "Our security teams are stretched to the limit with the rioting, and meanwhile we can't find the captain."

"You have no idea where he is?"

"All those leads were dead ends. He's disap-peared into thin air. And I don't mind telling you we need him here, now, or Commander Ivanova if he stays lost. There may be trouble in the Euphrates sector at any second.''

Ivanova took the link from Garibaldi. ''Is that ship back in position in hyperspace?''

''Yes,'' Zack said.

''Get it out of hyperspace and into orbit over our general position. Tell it to be ready to pick us up at a minute's notice.''

''Right,'' Zack complied.

''And double up on the search for Captain Sheridan. That's priority one. Turn whole docking bays into holding cells if you have to, but get the rioting under control so you can turn all your attention to the captain and Delenn.''

''Got you.''

''And hang in there, Zack.''

''That's the part I can't give you a promise on,'' Zack said, and signed off.

''Well, that's that.'' Ivanova handed the link back to Garibaldi. ''We're going home.''

''If we can just find our way back . . .'' Franklin said.

Garibaldi said, ''I think it was left, left, right, left . . .''

Ivanova protested, ''No, it was right, left, right, right . . .''

Sighing, Franklin followed, wishing he had left a trail of peas to get them out.

At the third or fourth turn to the right, they came upon something new: a narrowing in the tunnel, with steel walls replacing rock.

"We definitely made a wrong turn," Ivanova declared.

"Yep," Garibaldi admitted, turning around.

There was sudden movement, and they were confronted with an armed Narn. When they turned, another was there, trapping them.

A third Narn pushed his way past the second, brandishing his sword. "Well, what have we here?" he said.

Ivanova replied, "We're humans in disguise, not Centauri!"

Momentarily, the Narn looked startled.

Garibaldi stepped forward. "Actually, I can explain—"

The Narn stepped forward and struck him, driving him to the ground.

"Maybe later," Garibaldi mumbled.

"We're not who we seem to be. You see, we've come from G'Kar—" Franklin offered.

"Were you with him recently?"

"Yes."

"We know who the three of you are!" the Narn cried. "You're the dogs who returned G'Kar to the murderer Cartagia! And here you've walked right into us—how convenient!"

"Actually, we were looking for you—" Garibaldi said.

Ra'Nik kicked him where he lay, and the security chief was silent.

Behind this third Narn, a fourth pushed his way through. "What is it, Ra'Nik?" he said; then he saw the three new prisoners.

"They are the ones who kidnapped, then returned, G'Kar," Ra'Nik reported.

L'Kan held out his hands in mock glee.

"Welcome!" he sneered. "To your own executions!"

CHAPTER 56

It was becoming difficult to breathe.

"What will happen," Sheridan said, using as little oxygen as possible to speak, "is that eventually we'll go to sleep and won't wake up. Our brains will die from oxygen deprivation."

"That is not a pleasant thought, John," Delenn admitted.

"We've got to find a way out of this container."

"Either that," Delenn said, already sounding sleepy, "or we've got to find a way to get more air in."

Even with his fuzzy mind, Sheridan came to attention. "What did you say?"

"I said, we either get out, or bring more air in."

"Exactly . . ."

Sheridan had been working on his bonds since they had been loaded into the container. He knew that it was imperative that he free himself to have any chance of surviving.

"Almost . . . got it . . ."

Finally, he was able to work the ropes loose from

his wrists. Quickly, he began to work on Delenn's bonds, all the while admonishing her to stay awake.

"Delenn! Don't go to sleep on me!"

"I thought we mustn't speak . . ." she murmured sleepily.

Sheridan yanked at her wrist ropes, making her yelp.

"That hurt!"

"Stay awake! I've got an idea!"

"I knew you would come up with something, Agent Y," she yawned.

In a moment he had her loose, and then he was fumbling below him, at the boxes contained in the cargo crate with them.

"If we're in luck, we'll live," he said hopefully, ripping one of the boxes open in the dark and then examining the contents with his fingers in the dark.

The box was filled with stuffed teddy bears.

"No good," Sheridan said, fumbling for another.

"What are you doing?" Delenn asked, yawning again.

"Looking for oxygen."

Once more he examined the contents of the latest box, then tossed it aside in disgust when he felt only dolls.

"We've got two more chances to live," he announced, tearing open one of the two remaining containers.

A multitude of large, light, glass balls tumbled out.

"Eureka!" Sheridan cried, immediately breaking one of the balls between his palms.

"What—?" Delenn said dreamily, as a burst of fresh air puffed into the container.

"Each of them has oxygen trapped inside! Hurry! Help me!" Sheridan insisted, laughing in the dark as he broke another globe. The glass, an extremely lightweight plasti-mixture, tinkled into harmless evaporation as life-giving oxygen was released.

Delenn, waking up slightly, reached into the darkness, her hand brushing John's arm. John put a ball into her hand.

"I remember these objects!" she cried.

"Then help me!" Sheridan urged.

Soon they had exhausted the entire supply of glass spheres—but the air within the sealed container had been obviously refreshed.

"It won't give us forever, but it will give us more time."

Delenn was silent.

"What are you thinking?" Sheridan asked.

"Toys . . ." Delenn said, thoughtfully.

Sheridan laughed. "Obviously, toys. We're surrounded by them."

"Exactly," Delenn said suddenly, and John heard something ripping. It sounded almost as if Delenn were ripping apart a teddy bear.

She took his hand, placed something small in his palm. He examined it with his fingers. It was a computer chip. "Inside the toys?"

"These are firing parts for very large weapons," Delenn explained. "If we can—"

Sheridan hugged her in the darkness. "If we can

put the right ones together, we can make our own little bomb!''

"Yes," Delenn agreed, sounding breathless. "And if we do not blow ourselves up—then we will be free."

CHAPTER 57

A FEW minutes to live.

That's what the Narns had told him, a few minutes ago. As with everything, the Narns were not on time and did not do what they swore they would do when they would do it. Which annoyed Londo Mollari—but gave him a few seconds more to have his last thoughts.

Very well. He would meet death with a steady hand and with head held high.

As to his life . . .

Londo Mollari found that now, as he reviewed his life, there was not much he saw that he liked.

There were triumphs, yes. There was the raid he had led on Phalos 12, when he had been very young—and very naive.

There was the acquisition of the Eye—which, of course, had been stolen for a while—but having the Eye, itself, had been a triumph.

There was the return of the Centauri to greatness—the victory against the Narns.

There were other pleasant moments: his gambling winnings, though more meager than he would have

liked; his first wife—at least for that brief, first time
he had heard her voice and known momentary happiness without the bondage of arranged marriages.

There were other things: his first hangover, for
instance; other fleeting things here and there.

And then there were the things he didn't like.

The three wives, for instance.

And Lord Refa, whose treachery was legion.

And Morden, the Shadow-zombie with whom
Londo had signed his deal with the devil.

And, at this moment, Vir, who had seemed to
show promise, but now, in the end, proved that he
was not up to the tasks at hand and had failed in
freeing Londo from captivity and so preserving the
larger plan. Londo imagined Vir at this moment ag-
onizing over his arranged marriage to Lyndisty,
wallowing in his own misery, forgetting all about his
mentor Londo and the glory that would have ensued
had Londo and G'Kar's plan gone forward.

Londo spat: might Vir's marriage be a long—and
miserable—one.

And G'Kar . . .

Even now, as he waited for his life to end, Londo
found hatred welling up within him for the former
Narn ambassador to Babylon 5. Even though the
Narn and he had been so recently bound in their
plans to rid the Centauri Republic of Emperor
Cartagia, Londo still felt bile whenever G'Kar's face
rose into view.

Rose into view . . .

The one thing that puzzled Londo was that, in his
dreams, it had been foretold that G'Kar would be the
one to kill him. Was this, in reality, what the dream

meant? For, in a way, though the hated Narn's hands would not, this night, wrap themselves tightly around Londo's neck, were not G'Kar's hands just as simply causing the act of his death?

Were not the five Narn commandos who would soon come in and slit his throat acting as the hands of G'Kar?

Was this what his dreams meant?

Who knew . . .

At this point, who cared . . .

He was as ready as he would ever be for death.

There was a sound outside the room where he had been held captive. He shouted out, "All right, come in and kill me! I'm ready for you, you swine!"

He was so resigned to his death that he merely closed his eyes, held his head up proudly, and even bared his neck for the blade that the Narn assassins would now slice across it.

Time went by. He heard movement, but nothing happened.

"I said, cut my throat, you fools!"

"Don't tempt me, Londo," came a familiar voice.

"Garibaldi?" Londo answered in shock and wonder.

He opened his eyes.

Further shock: there were three unknown Centauri being tied to chairs by three of the Narns, who then left.

"You attempted to save me?" Londo said to the three bound Centauri, imperiously.

"Something like that," one of the Centauri, the woman, said—in another familiar voice.

"Commander . . . *Ivanova*?"

"In person," Ivanova said.

"What is . . . going on?" Londo said. His quick mind now was running through possibilities.

"Did Vir send you?" he asked.

"No," Garibaldi said. "G'Kar did."

"G'Kar?" Londo responded. "And where is G'Kar?"

"Well," Garibaldi explained, "actually, we freed him, and then he made us bring him back."

"Amazing," Londo said. With renewed hope he added, "Then the Narns will let me go? They believe that G'Kar must stay in captivity?"

"Not exactly," Ivanova said. "Though we told them who we are, they seem to have gotten it into their heads that we're traitors to Narn."

"But you're not Centauri!" Londo said.

"True," Garibaldi said. "And we told them that too, but it doesn't seem to matter. The only thing that matters to them is that we sprung G'Kar and then brought him back."

"But you are from Babylon 5! They cannot treat you this way!"

"In their minds they can. I even let them talk to Zack back on the station. Didn't matter. They took a vow, and that's that."

"But what are they going to do with you?" Londo asked.

"Well," Garibaldi said, "at the moment, it seems that they have four executions planned tonight, instead of just one."

CHAPTER 58

"Here goes nothing, Agent X," Sheridan warned.

"I'm ready when you are, Agent Y," Delenn answered.

Ambassador Delenn was crouched at one end of the container, covered with boxes and toys to shield her from the planned detonation.

It had taken Sheridan nearly all of their new supply of air to rig up something using three distinct detonator components found in the toys. And even now he didn't know how powerful the coming blast would be.

"One of four things will happen," Sheridan determined, steeling himself. He had covered himself in as much detritus as possible, and constructed a wall of boxes and toys in front of the detonating device he had built, but the fact was that he had to activate it himself and was closer than Delenn. "One: Nothing will happen, in which case we'll be dead in a matter of minutes from carbon dioxide poisoning. Two: The blast will be too great, and blow us to smithereens. Three: The blast won't be powerful enough, and will leave us to die knowing we tried . . .''

"I get the feeling I will like number four the best," Delenn said.

"Four: The blast is just large enough to blow open the seal on this container and get us out.

"In that case, though," Sheridan continued, "we won't have time to congratulate ourselves. Mitchell and his friends are bound to hear the explosion, and they'll be on us before you know it. We'll still have to be ready to fight when we get out. If we get out."

"I like 'when' better than 'if,' " Delenn said, yawning.

"Time to do this—ready?" Sheridan asked.

"Ready, Agent Y," she answered.

"Here goes nothing." Sheridan reached tentatively through his wall until his finger rested on the makeshift detonator he had constructed.

He pushed it.

Nothing happened.

"Great—" Sheridan began in disappointment.

At that moment there was a hiss, followed by a booming sound.

Sheridan found himself blinded by light and flying through the air. He saw Delenn out of the corner of his eye likewise being thrown free of the container.

With an *oomph,* Sheridan landed on a pile of boxes, which split open.

Dolls spilled out.

He heard movement.

"Delenn, are you all right?" he called.

"Remarkably, yes, I am," she said, appearing

from behind another pile of boxes as the door to the cargo hold slid back and Mitchell rushed in.

Delenn was closest to him and thrust out an arm, which caught him in the throat.

He went down.

Behind him was the giant, who hesitated and then came into the room, stepping over the gagging ringleader.

But Sheridan was ready for him, and as the giant bounded into the hold the captain rose behind him, kicking the man behind the knees and sending him down. He then karate-chopped the giant on the back of the neck, and the man was still.

"Just like James Bond!" Sheridan laughed.

The short man was entering, aiming a PPG gun at Sheridan when Delenn tossed a teddy bear to him.

"Catch!" she yelled, and when the small man hesitated she was on him, chopping the gun from his wrist and then driving him to the ground with another blow. She turned as Mitchell rose to his feet. Delenn raised her index and pinkie fingers Minbari-style and hit him once more in the neck, dropping him again.

"Very good!" Sheridan congratulated. "Let's see if we can find something to tie them up with!"

In no time the three culprits were tied hand and foot and gagged. With relish, the captain had tied a doll to each of them.

"To keep you company, until we can get you into the brig on Babylon 5," he said.

In wonder, Delenn and Sheridan examined the

container that had been their prison. The sealed seam had broken all along one side, spitting them out with the explosion as if they had been peas. The gaping hole looked like a mouth.

Delenn reached within the open cavity, rummaged around, and came up with a teddy bear from inside.

"I think I shall keep this as a souvenir," she said.

"Spies don't need souvenirs!" Sheridan protested.

"And I think," Delenn continued, "that from this moment on, I shall no longer be a spy."

"But Agent X, how could you do this to me!"

Delenn held up her finger. "No. From now on, Agent X is retired. From now on, she is just Ambassador Delenn."

"But—!"

"And you," she said, "are now Captain John Sheridan again. Which is enough for me."

"I guess you're right," the captain ceded, realizing that they had plenty to do, and that the first priority was to check in with Babylon 5 to see what had happened during his captivity. "But I'll sure miss the thrill."

"I thought this was supposed to be a game? A . . . vacation?"

"Well . . ." Sheridan smiled. "Let's just say it got a little exciting."

"That excitement," Delenn declared, surveying the damage around them, and the three criminals bound up in one corner of the hold, "is something I will definitely *not* miss."

CHAPTER 59

THOUGH Vir was not afraid, he was still timid.

How did one mount a rescue mission—especially if one didn't know how to rescue anyone?

He decided the best thing to do was just go.

He soon found himself skulking through a maze of tunnels, following the map he had been given as if there were buried treasure at the other end.

Which, in a way, there was.

And then, the more he proceeded, the more his confidence grew.

After all, even if he died tonight, at least he'd die true to himself, wouldn't he?

He'd been honest with Lyndisty, hadn't he?

And then, suddenly, he felt almost invincible.

Maybe he *wouldn't* die tonight after all! Maybe his forthrightness with Lyndisty had been a sign. Maybe *all* of his problems would go away tonight!

Hearing a sound, he hid behind a turn in the tunnel wall.

The sound repeated, and cautiously, he looked around the corner.

A bengi-bat flew at him, all red eyes and snapping teeth and claws.

"Yuch!" he cried out, loud enough to be heard throughout the tunnel system, and swatted the chirping creature away.

Another followed, and another—he was nearly covered in the repulsive creatures.

He swatted his way through them, exclaiming his disgust, and moved on.

He hadn't been warned about the bats—if he got out of this alive maybe he *wouldn't* pay that bonus after all . . .

Time went by. Consulting his map, he moved this way and that through the tunnel system, growing ever closer to his goal, moving, in his mind, like a wraith though the night—

Yes, that was it! He was a wraith! The most secretive of Centauri, able to be invisible when needed, moving like the wind and striking like a hammer blow. He was a superbeing! Invincible! Unflappable!

He tripped over an unseen rise in the rock flooring, and went tumbling end over end, hitting his head.

"Owwwww . . ." he complained, sitting up and rubbing at his head.

Well, perhaps not a wraith.

He fumbled in his tunic for the map and couldn't find it.

In the weak light, he padded the ground with his hands and finally located it. It had flown loose when he had fallen on his face . . .

Some superbeing.

He studied the map carefully, rose, and walked on.

Turn, after turn, after turn . . .

Another sound up ahead; according to the map, he was getting close . . .

Amazing—all five Narns, together and moving away!

Vir consulted his map—yes, sure enough, the room where Londo was being held was up ahead—and now unguarded!

Stuffing the map into his cloak, Vir crept ahead, and stopped, unbreathing, while the five Narns, talking among themselves, moved off and were gone.

He darted ahead, straight for the room the map said contained Londo.

He threw open the door.

"Londo!" he cried out, in a fierce, expectant whisper.

The room was empty. A mining storage area with nothing in it but stored equipment. It had not been used in some time, it was obvious.

Definitely no bonus, he thought; Chilo could be buried upside down in a vegetable field, for all Vir cared at the moment . . .

He heard a noise from an adjoining room.

More than one voice?

Puzzled, Vir pushed aside some boxes until a door to the adjoining chamber was revealed.

He opened it and peered into a darkened space.

"Londo?" he queried timidly.

"Vir—is that you?" came an amazed voice.

"Yes!"

"There is a switch along the far wall to activate

the lights,'' Londo ordered. ''How did you get here?''

''It's a long story,'' Vir said, as he began to make his way tentatively through the darkened room. He hit one object that said, ''Hey!'' in a voice he knew.

''Mr. Garibaldi?'' Vir gasped in wonder.

''The same.''

''Hello, Vir,'' came Dr. Franklin's voice; and then, in further amazement, Vir heard Commander Ivanova say, ''Me, too, Vir.''

''What are you all doing here?'' Vir demanded, bumping into another shape, which proved to be Londo.

''Never mind the questions until you find the lights!'' Londo snapped peevishly.

Finally, Vir found the indicated switch, and the room was flooded with light.

And was occupied by Londo—

And three Centauri!

CHAPTER 60

"I CAN'T *believe* that story—and I can't *believe* what you've done for G'Kar—and Londo!" Vir remarked, as he freed the last of the four captives by loosening the bonds on Mr. Garibaldi's hands.

"You didn't do so bad yourself, Vir," Garibaldi commented, standing and rubbing at his wrists.

Vir was studying him closely.

"What is it?" Garibaldi asked.

Vir squinted. "It's just that when the doctor applied his disguise, he missed a few small details. For instance—"

"Vir!" Londo cried. "That's irrelevant at the moment!" To the others he said, "I suggest we get out of here."

"Unfortunately," Garibaldi admitted, "the Narns took my link, and I can't communicate with the ship waiting for us. We'll have to wing it."

"Just get us all out of here," Londo ordered impatiently, "and I'll get you a hundred links. I suggest we go!"

Ivanova led them to the storage area where Vir had broken through to them. "Looks good in here," she said, and they followed her into the room and then to its door.

Out in the passageway, there was approaching sound.

Ivanova ducked back into the room as the group of Narns passed.

"We're going to have to run for it," Ivanova cautioned.

"We can do that," Garibaldi answered, and now he hurried the others out into the passage ahead of him.

They sprinted as a group until they reached the first split in the tunnels.

"Left or right?" Ivanova asked.

Garibaldi was about to answer when Vir said, "I have a map . . ."

He fumbled in his clothing and came up empty.

"Where is it?" Londo demanded.

"It was here . . ." Vir moaned. "And I paid good money for it, too . . ."

"Left," Garibaldi directed.

They turned left and moved on.

At the next turn, as Vir still padded his clothing, looking for the map, Ivanova said, "Now we turn right."

At the next, Garibaldi led them; then Ivanova in turn.

They turned a corner as Vir suddenly crowed in triumph: "Got it!" and pulled his piece of parchment from his cloak.

They stood staring.

"I don't believe it," Ivanova groaned.

Vir said, "I guess I was a bit late?"

They stood right back where they had started—
and now the Narns were there, waiting, weapons
drawn.

CHAPTER 61

"THE only difference," L'Kan said, "is that now there will be five executions instead of four."

Beside him, Ra'Nik nodded.

"But you must believe me!" Vir insisted. He was now tied to his own chair. They had brought him into a separate chamber to interrogate him while the others resumed their former positions bound to chairs in the original prison.

L'Kan, pacing, fumed, "And why should we believe you, when we do not believe the others?" He ticked off on his fingers: "First, we have Londo Mollari, who would lie about anything at any time, telling us that G'Kar must stay in captivity." He ticked off three more fingers. "Then we find ourselves with three meddling humans, disguised as Centauri, who actually kidnap G'Kar for their own purposes, and then sell him back into captivity! They *also* claim G'Kar must stay in captivity. And they claim to be our friends!"

"They *are* your friends!"

"They are traitors! And will die as Centauri, along with the rest of you!"

"But—"

"And then we have *you*," L'Kan snarled, balling his fist except for a single pointing finger, which he jabbed at Vir's chest in passing, making Cotto wince.

"Yes, me . . ." Vir muttered.

"You followed none of your instructions from us, you went your own way, just like a Centauri— and now you expect us to believe that everything *you* say is true!"

"But it is!"

Ra'Nik scoffed. "He has a plan." He came close to Vir, peering into his face. "They *always* have a plan."

"My plan is to help save your homeworld!" Vir pleaded. "Isn't that what you want?"

"Our mission was to free G'Kar," L'Kan retorted, still thinking. "In that we have failed."

"In that you *must* fail! But you'll be doing greater good for Narn if you just go home and forget all about us!"

L'Kan pondered again, scowling. "We will go home, because we have failed—but we will not forget about you."

"Does that mean—" Vir began, showing relief.

"We will remember your deaths," L'Kan pronounced. He signaled to Ra'Nik as he stalked out of the room. "Prepare the five of them for execution."

CHAPTER 62

"CAPTAIN Sheridan!" Zack said, not able to hide the surprise in his voice. "I can't tell you how good it is to hear from you!"

"I feel good about it myself," Sheridan said.

"Where are you?" Zack's voice inquired, as Sheridan sat in the cockpit of the makeshift freighter that had been, until an hour ago, on its way to Mars.

"We're just out of the Epsilon jump gate. In fact, we'll be home before you know it. With three prisoners. How are things?"

"Well, the rioting got pretty serious as soon as you disappeared, but in the last few hours we finally got things calmed down. You know, your timing is pretty good, Captain."

Sheridan glanced at Delenn. "I wish I could take credit for that."

"What exactly happened to you?" Zack asked.

Sheridan told a quick version of what had occurred.

"And Ambassador Delenn is all right?" Zack said.

"She's fine. And just as anxious as I am to get back to Babylon 5."

"Is there anything you need, Captain?"

"Yes. For now, I want a docking bay and I want to know two things. First of all, how have things been in the Euphrates sector?"

"Quiet again, lately."

"Good. And what news do you have from Ivanova and the others?"

"No news at all, sir."

"What!"

"There was a ship waiting for their signal, but it hasn't heard from them."

"I'll handle it as soon as I get in."

"Yes, sir."

"And Zack," the captain said. "Sounds like you did a good job while I was . . . indisposed."

"Thank you, Captain. And Captain?"

"Yes, Zack?"

"Thanks for coming back."

Sheridan laughed.

CHAPTER 63

"Any last wishes?" L'Kan taunted, with sarcasm.

"Yes," Londo spat. "I wish I wasn't here—and I wish you were dead instead of me."

"Comical to the last, Mollari."

"You know," Garibaldi said, "you're making a big mistake."

"Save your breath," L'Kan sneered. "I thought long and hard about your involvement in this venture. I still don't understand it—but then, we Narns have not understood your human response since the Centauri have started to rape and pillage our world with the Shadows' help. You profess sorrow, and yet you only engaged the Shadows when it suited your purposes. The Narn homeworld lay in ruins by that time, and our people enslaved. And yet . . . neutrality I can tolerate—but not active collaboration. When you kidnapped G'Kar from Cartagia, you had a chance to prove yourselves worthy of our friendship. Instead, you gave him back—for whatever foolish reasons you have. I suspect they are political or monetary. Perhaps Cartagia has pledged to get the Shadows to spare Babylon 5? Perhaps he gave you riches? After all, we found a few gem-stones on you when you were captured.''

"We told you, we were posing as jewel mer-chants!" Franklin snapped in exasperation.

L'Kan held up his hand. "The reasons are incom-prehensible. If you think I would execute three hu-man members of Babylon 5 for frivolous reasons, you are wrong. I have thought seriously on this mat-ter, and can come to no other conclusion than that you are collaborators with the Centauri. So the mat-ter must end as it does."

He nodded to Ra'Nik, who signalled to the other three Narn.

Each of the five of them drew his *ka'toc*.

"Oh, boy." Garibaldi flinched.

"You mean you're just getting worried now?" Ivanova asked.

"When they take out the *ka'toc,* they can't put it back until it has blood on it," Garibaldi said.

"So we can assume they're serious?"

"Assume all you want," Garibaldi quipped. "In my book, we're dead meat."

The five Narn advanced on their prisoners, each tied to a chair side by side.

"It will be as painless as possible," L'Kan an-nounced, advancing on Mollari. Each of you will be stabbed once, in the most vital region which will bring quick death. *Except for Mollari.*"

"Wonderful," Mollari moaned. "Many days of bad food and aching buttocks, followed by a slow death."

When the five were a sword's length away, Vir cried out, "Wait!"

The Narns momentarily hesitated, and L'Kan turned to face the younger Centauri. "What is it, fool?"

"I object to the fool part, but I wanted to ask if it might be possible for you to kill only me."

"Just *you*?"

"Yes," Vir said. "Kill me, and let the others live."

"Even Mollari?"

"Especially Mollari!" Vir replied earnestly. "If he lives, he and G'Kar will be able to carry out their plan, and save your homeworld. Along with mine."

L'Kan actually looked puzzled. After a moment's thought, he stepped over to Vir, gently pushing the executioner who was to kill the Centauri aside. He brought his *ka'toc* under Vir's chin.

"You know that I have already killed Centauri with this sword, do you not?"

"I know that," Vir responded, as fearlessly as he could manage.

The sword flicked out, and suddenly there was a slight cut under Vir's chin, which bled in a thin line.

"You are willing to die for the others?" L'Kan demanded.

Trembling, but holding the other's gaze, Vir gulped and sputtered, "I am."

"Even for Mollari?"

"Yes."

L'Kan stood solemnly, stared off into a far place for a moment, and then turned to his compatriots.

"We must speak," he said.

The five Narn retreated to an adjoining room.

While they were gone Mollari and the others turned to Vir.

"Vir, what are you doing!" Mollari said. "Do you realize what you have said? You would truly sacrifice your life for me?"

"Not only for you, Londo," Vir said. "For your plan. For what must be done."

"Are you sure you are Centauri?" Londo said, shaking his head in wonder.

The five Narn returned. Ra'Nik, followed by the three underlings, advanced on Vir, swords held steady before them.

Behind them, arms folded, L'Kan spoke up. "Any regrets, Vir Cotto?"

Vir, eyes wide on the four swords advancing on him, gulped again and said, "Plenty! But—I meant what I said."

"Vir, you must not do this!" Londo shouted, as the three humans protested as well.

"No—do what you must," Vir said to the Narn leader.

"Very well," L'Kan ceded.

The four advanced on Vir, a look of determination on their faces. As one they drew their swords back . . .

CHAPTER 64

CAPTAIN John Sheridan, safely in command again, stood at Command and Control in the Observation Dome of Babylon 5 and, hands clasped behind his back, said, "Have they gotten the order?"

"The ship is moving out of hyperspace toward Centauri Prime now," came the reply from a junior officer.

"And they understand what they're to do?"

"Acknowledged, Captain. They will land at the rendezvous point and wait there."

"And if they're questioned by Centauri authorities?"

"Their cover story is still in place, Captain. They will say they are a diplomatic mission from Babylon 5 and that they developed thruster trouble. It will give them a couple of hours at least."

"Good." Staring out through the dome into space, the captain said, "I only wish I was there with Ivanova, Garibaldi, and Franklin. And I pray to God they're safe."

CHAPTER 65

As Mollari shouted, "No!" and as Garibaldi, Franklin, and Ivanova called out their own protests, each of the four Narn in turn stepped up to Vir Cotto, who had bravely bared his neck while closing his eyes, and each of four *ka'toc* swords gently nicked the Centauri under the chin, drawing a tiny drop of blood.

As the four Narn stepped back, Vir cautiously cocked one eye open.

"I'm alive?" he asked, tentatively.

L'Kan said, "Very much so." He motioned to his four compatriots, who stepped forward to loosen the bonds of all the prisoners. L'Kan himself freed Vir Cotto and helped him to his feet.

Vir dabbed with a finger at the nicks under his chin and said, "Oooo! That hurts!"

He noted that the Narn leader was regarding him with admiration.

"Why am I still alive?" Vir said, and quickly added, "Not that I'm complaining or anything . . ."

"Because you have honor—and because what you

said must be true. The fact is that no Centauri would ever sacrifice himself for another. Until you were truly willing to die, I could not believe you. But the inescapable fact is that the cause you spoke of must truly be greater than your own life. I get the feeling that if Londo Mollari were in your spot, he would have reneged at the last moment to save his miserable life—"

Here L'Kan looked at Londo, who began with some scorn, "Do I look like a fool?" He then stopped himself and said, "We'll never know that, will we?"

"Then you believe me?" Vir said to L'Kan.

To Vir's great surprise, the Narn put a hand on his shoulder. "Yes. It can only be the truth that G'Kar must stay in captivity for a greater reason. And now that I have made this decision, it is only reasonable that the three from Babylon 5 must be telling the truth, also."

Ivanova nodded. "Believe me, we are."

L'Kan said, "My only regret is that we are unable to cut Mollari's throat."

"Well, you could," Vir said, in some rush, "but that would ruin the plan to free Narn—wait, that didn't come out right . . ."

"Vir!" Londo shouted.

"If you're through with us," Garibaldi interjected, "we really should go. If you could give us back our equipment, I should contact the ship that will get us off this planet before Cartagia's imperial guards get hold of us."

"Of course," L'Kan said.

"I suggest," Londo proposed haughtily, "that everything that has happened here be kept secret."

"As far as I'm concerned," Ivanova said, "none of it ever happened."

Vir said, "Agreed." He turned to L'Kan, who nodded also.

"Can we give you a lift somewhere?" Garibaldi asked the Narn leader.

"As a matter of fact, there is a staging point that we need to get to, if we are to get off Centauri Prime. If you could . . ."

"I would be happy to guarantee your safety myself," Londo said. "Just to get rid of you—"

L'Kan interrupted, "We will go with Mr. Garibaldi and his friends." His face hardened as he regarded Londo. "And I wish to give you a bit of warning, Mollari. If we ever meet again, after the matters at hand are resolved, I will kill you myself."

"You needn't bother," Mollari sneered. "For I will do everything in my power to make sure that we never meet again. And besides, my death will not be at your hand. Let's just say someone you know is involved . . ."

L'Kan regarded the Centauri coolly for a moment, and then turned away. "I suggest we all have places to be," he said.

"I will leave by myself," Londo proclaimed, stalking out.

As Vir made to follow, L'Kan once again did an unexpected thing: he put his arm around the Centauri's shoulder.

"Are you sure, Vir Cotto," L'Kan marveled in all earnestness, "that you are not part Narn?"

CHAPTER 66

In a soundproof briefing room on Babylon 5, a secret meeting was held.

Captain John Sheridan called the meeting to order. With him sat Commander Susan Ivanova, Security Chief Michael Garibaldi, Dr. Stephen Franklin, and Minbari Ambassador Delenn.

"You all know why we're here," the captain began. "I just want to reiterate what we all know already: that is, that our recent . . . escapades, for obvious reasons, must be kept secret."

There was no dissent.

The captain allowed himself a slight smile. "I must also confess that my own days as a secret agent are over—even though Ambassador Delenn and I *were* able to break up a covert weapons-smuggling operation . . ."

Delenn allowed herself her own smile. "Agent Y, I think we must allow for the presence of luck in our 'secret agent' operation."

"True, Agent X," Sheridan said.

"I, for one, won't be reading any more James Bond adventures," Garibaldi acknowledged.

"Oh, I don't know," Sheridan cajoled. "Didn't you find it exciting to be involved in a secret mission?"

Ivanova tilted her head. "I'll find it more exciting to get my own hair back."

Franklin examined her head. "That wig you're wearing now isn't *too* bad, is it? It looks just like your real hair."

"It'll do for now—but it itches!"

There was general laughter.

"This meeting," Sheridan said, "is now adjourned. And remember—it never happened."

"Then why does my scalp itch?" Ivanova said.

CHAPTER 67

G'KAR concentrated on one thought: the Narn homeworld. He found that if he thought as hard as he could about the devastated cities, the red, ashen sky, the destruction, he could somehow envision the way it might someday look. If he thought of the Narn people as slaves, as a people beaten down, he could somehow see them restored again to greatness. In other words, if he thought of things at their worst, it was easy to think that they might soon get better.

Also, it was a way to deaden the pain . . .

"It is amazing to me," Cartagia said from his red throne, "that even a Narn could take so much pain!"

Once again the lash came across G'Kar's bare back. Once again his thoughts went beyond hate to think of his homeworld—and what soon might happen . . .

* * *

Vir Cotto, to his surprise and delight, found that he was about to have the unequaled luxury of getting a good night's sleep in his own bed.

How recently did this seem like an impossible dream! By all measure, he should be dead now—or something worse, in the grasp of Lyndisty's marriage plans!

But now—both of these problems were magically gone!

Londo was home, and safe, his plan with G'Kar back on track; and Lyndisty, no doubt, would never forgive him for his actions the night of her gala—

Remarkable! It was truly remarkable!

She would probably never speak to him again!

A smile of contentment on his face, Vir settled into his covers and closed his eyes. Fragments of what had happened the past few days drifted inside his head, trying to connect but happily remaining formless as he dropped into sleep . . .

And then a dream came to him: he was in his bedchamber, in his bed, when a rustle of the curtains took on form and Lyndisty's voice said, "Vir? Can you hear me?"

In the dream, he tried to hide beneath the covers, but she came into the room, peeled the covers back, and smiled at him sweetly.

"Vir, dear! We just heard what you did, how you saved Londo Mollari's life! I must say, my parents and I were so confused the night of the gala, the way you acted—Vir, I couldn't understand any of it and I cried so! I thought our marriage was never to be! But now that we've learned the news, and know why you acted like you did—why, everything's changed!

You're a hero, Vir! And my parents have a higher regard for you than ever before! And so do I, dear Vir!''

As Vir tried to tunnel deeper into the bedclothes, Lyndisty said enticingly, ''And that's why my parents have rescheduled their gala for you—and it will be even bigger than before—''

Vir awoke with a shout, covered in cold sweat.

Such a horrible nightmare!

Even now, sitting up in bed, he was shivering . . .

The curtains were rustling—and one of them, he now saw in horror, held a form that stepped out from behind it.

And then Lyndisty's alluring voice called, ''Vir?''

The Babylon 5 Series

Based on the Hit Television Series by J. Michael Straczynski

Babylon 5 © and ™ 1997 Warner Bros.

850397 Dell